American Pie

American Pie represents the most commercially successful example of the vulgar teen comedy, and this book analyses the film's development, audience-appeal and cultural significance.

American Pie (1999) is a film that exemplifies the most disparaged of movie genres – the vulgar teen comedy. Largely aimed at young audiences, the vulgar teen comedy is characterised by a brazenly over-the-top humour rooted in the salacious, the scatological and the squirmingly tasteless.

In this book, consideration is given to the relationship between *American Pie*'s success and broad shifts within both the youth market and the film business. Attention is also given to the film's representations of youth, gender and sexuality, together with the distinctive character of its comedy and the enduring place of such humour in contemporary popular culture. While chiefly focusing on the original *American Pie* movie, the book also considers the development of the franchise, with discussion of the movie's three sequels and four direct-to-DVD releases. The book also charts the history, nature and appeal of vulgar teen comedy as a whole, providing the first concerted analysis of this generally overlooked category of youth film.

Clear, concise and comprehensive, the book is ideal for students, scholars and general readership worldwide.

Bill Osgerby is Emeritus Professor of Media, Culture and Communication at London Metropolitan University. He has published widely on twentieth-century British and American cultural history. His books include *Youth in Britain Since 1945* and *Youth Media*.

Cinema and Youth Cultures
Series Editors: Siân Lincoln & Yannis Tzioumakis

Cinema and Youth Cultures engages with well-known youth films from American cinema as well as the cinemas of other countries. Using a variety of methodological and critical approaches the series volumes provide informed accounts of how young people have been represented in film, while also exploring the ways in which young people engage with films made for and about them. In doing this, the Cinema and Youth Cultures series contributes to important and long-standing debates about youth cultures, how these are mobilized and articulated in influential film texts and the impact that these texts have had on popular culture at large.

The Virgin Suicides
Justin Wyatt

The Breakfast Club
Elissa H. Nelson

The Freshman
Christina G. Petersen

Y Tu Mamá También
Scott L. Baugh

Halloween
Mark Bernard

American Pie
Bill Osgerby

For more information about this series, please visit: https://www.routledge.com/Cinema-and-Youth-Cultures/book-series/CYC

American Pie
The Anatomy of Vulgar Teen Comedy

Bill Osgerby

There's something about your first piece.

Routledge
Taylor & Francis Group

LONDON AND NEW YORK

First published 2020
by Routledge
2 Park Square, Milton Park, Abingdon, Oxon OX14 4RN

and by Routledge
605 Third Avenue, New York, NY 10017

First issued in paperback 2021

Routledge is an imprint of the Taylor & Francis Group, an informa business

British Library Cataloguing-in-Publication Data
A catalogue record for this book is available from the British Library

Library of Congress Cataloging-in-Publication Data
Names: Osgerby, Bill, author.
Title: American pie: the anatomy of vulgar teen comedy / Bill Osgerby.
Description: London; New York: Routledge, 2020. |
Series: Cinema and youth cultures | Includes bibliographical
references and index.
Identifiers: LCCN 2019029779 (print) | LCCN 2019029780 (ebook) |
ISBN 9781138681941 (hardback) | ISBN 9781315545479 (ebook)
Subjects: LCSH: American pie (Motion picture) |
Teenagers in motion pictures. | Vulgarity in motion pictures |
Teen films—United States—History and criticism. |
Comedy films—United States—History and criticism.
Classification: LCC PN1997.A34325 O84 2020 (print) | LCC
PN1997.A34325 (ebook) | DDC 791.43/72—dc23
LC record available at https://lccn.loc.gov/2019029779
LC ebook record available at https://lccn.loc.gov/2019029780

ISBN 13: 978-1-03-208783-2 (pbk)
ISBN 13: 978-1-138-68194-1 (hbk)

Typeset in Times New Roman
by codeMantra

Contents

Figures

Series editors' introduction

Despite the high visibility of youth films in the global media marketplace, especially since the 1980s when Conglomerate Hollywood realized that such films were not only strong box office performers but also the starting point for ancillary sales in other media markets as well as for franchise building, academic studies that focused specifically on such films were slow to materialize. Arguably the most important factor behind academia's reluctance to engage with youth films was a (then) widespread perception within the Film and Media Studies communities that such films held little cultural value and significance, and therefore were not worthy of serious scholarly research and examination. Just like the young subjects they represented, whose interests and cultural practices have been routinely deemed transitional and transitory, so were the films that represented them perceived as fleeting and easily digestible, destined to be forgotten quickly, as soon as the next youth film arrived in cinema screens a week later.

Under these circumstances, and despite a small number of pioneering studies in the 1980s and early 1990s, the field of 'youth film studies' did not really start blossoming and attracting significant scholarly attention until the 2000s and in combination with similar developments in cognate areas such as 'girl studies.' However, because of the paucity of material in the previous decades, the majority of these new studies in the 2000s focused primarily on charting the field and therefore steered clear of long, in-depth examinations of youth films or was exemplified by edited collections that chose particular films to highlight certain issues to the detriment of others. In other words, despite providing often wonderfully rich accounts of youth cultures as these have been captured by key films, these studies could not have possibly dedicated sufficient space to engage with more than just a few key aspects of youth films.

In more recent (post-2010) years a number of academic studies started delimiting their focus and therefore providing more space for in-depth examinations of key types of youth films, such as slasher films and biker films or examining youth films in particular historical periods. From that point on, it was a matter of time for the first publications that focused exclusively on key youth films from a number of perspectives to appear (*Mamma Mia! The Movie*, *Twilight* and *Dirty Dancing* are among the first films to receive this treatment). Conceived primarily as edited collections, these studies provided a multifaceted analysis of these films, focusing on such issues as the politics of representing youth, the stylistic and narrative choices that characterize these films and the extent to which they are representative of a youth cinema, the ways these films address their audiences, the ways youth audiences engage with these films, the films' industrial location and other relevant issues.

It is within this increasingly maturing and expanding academic environment that the Cinema and Youth Cultures volumes arrive, aiming to consolidate existing knowledge, provide new perspectives, apply innovative methodological approaches, offer sustained and in-depth analyses of key films and therefore become the 'go to' resource for students and scholars interested in theoretically informed, authoritative accounts of youth cultures in film. As editors, we have tried to be as inclusive as possible in our selection of key examples of youth films by commissioning volumes on films that span the history of cinema, including the silent film era; that portray contemporary youth cultures as well as ones associated with particular historical periods; that represent examples of mainstream and independent cinema; that originate in American cinema and the cinemas of other nations; that attracted significant critical attention and commercial success during their initial release and that were 'rediscovered' after an unpromising initial critical reception. Together these volumes are going to advance youth film studies while also being able to offer extremely detailed examinations of films that are now considered significant contributions to cinema and our cultural life more broadly.

We hope readers will enjoy the series.

Siân Lincoln & Yannis Tzioumakis
Cinema & Youth Cultures Series Editors

Acknowledgements

I thank Yannis Tzioumakis and Siân Lincoln for inviting me to contribute this book to their *Cinema and Youth Studies* series. Their encouragement and feedback have been invaluable. I would also like to say a big 'thank you' to Jennifer Vennall and Natalie Foster at Routledge for their amazing patience and support.

I would especially like to thank Liz Davies for all her wonderful help, for reading through the manuscript and for laughing at the bits about the Stifmeister.

1 Serving up *American Pie*

Youth, cinema and vulgar teen comedy

'We will make a stand! We will succeed! We will get laid!'

American Pie is one of the foremost movies in the pantheon of vulgar teen comedy. Released by Universal Pictures in 1999, written by Adam Herz and the directorial debut for brothers Paul and Chris Weitz, the film stands as the epitome of vulgar teen comedy's stock-in-trade – an indefatigable enthusiasm for the lewd, the crude and the excruciatingly 'grossed out'.

The picture follows the knock-about antics and carnal misadventures of four high school buddies – the central character Jim Levenstein (Jason Biggs) and his friends Chris 'Oz' Ostreicher (Chris Klein), Kevin Myers (Thomas Ian Nicholas) and Paul Finch (Eddie Kaye Thomas) – who make a pact to defy their reputation as nerdy, sexual no-hopers by losing their virginity before graduation. As the foursome ruminate over their woeful lack of erotic experience, the challenge takes on the proportions of an intrepid quest. Momentarily shrugging off his dorky mantle, Kevin rouses his fellow adventurers with a speech worthy of an epic hero (See Figure 1.1). 'No longer will our penises remain flaccid and unused!', an indomitable Kevin avers:

> From now on, we fight for every man out there who isn't getting laid when he should be! This is our day! This is our time! And, by God, we're not gonna let history condemn us to celibacy! We will make a stand! We will succeed! We will get laid!

Along the way, the hapless quartet get incitement and impediment in equal measure from their erstwhile pal – the compellingly obnoxious anti-hero Steve Stifler (Seann William Scott). Self-mythologised as 'The Stifmeister', Stifler is distinguished by his leviathan ego, his gift for inventive profanity and his relentless (and somewhat improbable)

Figure 1.1 Kevin (Thomas Ian Nicholas) rouses his fellow adventurers – 'We will get laid!'

sexual braggadocio. 'You're a disgrace to men everywhere', the Stifmeister lectures his lackluster classmates:

> I mean, look at the Stifmeister. I got laid twenty-three times this year, and I'm not counting the hummer I got in the library stacks, baby.[1]

The title of *American Pie* is, perhaps, deceptively homely. The name is taken from folk rocker Don McLean's 1971 hit record, a bitter-sweet anthem to 1950s teen Americana, though screenwriter Herz has explained that it also refers to the quest of losing one's virginity in high school which, he argues, is 'as American as apple pie'.[2] But the title also nods towards one of the movie's principal set-piece jokes. After being assured by his (marginally) more experienced friends that sexual intimacy with a girl 'feels like warm apple pie', the eager (but lamentably naïve) Jim decides to rehearse his technique with one of his mother's freshly baked desserts. Sadly, as Jim's coitus with the pastry approaches climax, his cheery dad enters the kitchen – and the extraordinary scene freezes father and son (and the audience) in jaw-dropping mortification (see Figure 1.2).

Figure 1.2 Jim's dad (Eugene Levy) freezes in jaw-dropping mortification.

'The gross-out comedy that grossed large'

American Pie's zeal for infantile humour and its knack for plumbing the depths of bad taste ensured the film received some less than glowing reviews. Writing for the *New York Times*, for example, Stephen Holden judged that, among the year's 'crop of shallow teenage movies', *American Pie* represented 'the shallowest and the most prurient' (Holden, 1999). In a similar vein, Robert Horten, for *Film. com*, warned that although *American Pie* had 'a few amusing bits', the audience should 'strongly note that the movie is really awful' and 'not at all worthy of guilty pleasure status' (Horten, 1999). Others, however, have been more positive. Film scholar Robin Wood, for instance, has saluted *American Pie* as his favourite high school film of the 1990s; Wood arguing in a neat (but possibly unintended) *double entendre* that *American Pie* represented 'one of those rare films where "everything came together"':

> ...one has the impression that the actors really enjoyed themselves, that there was a constant sense of fun and pleasure in the making of the film, a communal creative engagement more pronounced than in any of the other films... The film is very funny, but also very *sweet*, generous to its characters and with a sort of seductive innocence.
>
> (Wood, 2003: 312)

Nor is Wood a voice in the wilderness. In 2000 readers of UK fan magazine *Total Film* voted *American Pie* sixth in a survey of 'The Greatest Comedies Ever' (Crook, 2000: 69). And in 2012 members of LoveFilm (a video streaming service subsequently subsumed into Amazon Prime) rated *American Pie* seventh in a poll of movies that had made them laugh the most, the film triggering an estimated 1.5 laughs per minute (Bender, 2012).[3] *American Pie*'s box office returns are also testimony to its audience popularity. The movie's domestic takings totaled a massive $102,561,004, while its foreign release garnered a further $132,922,000.[4] *American Pie* was, as film theorist Mandy Merck wryly observes, 'the gross-out comedy that grossed large' (Merck, 2007: 259).

Such bankability ensured a succession of *American Pie* sequels across the following decade. All chronicle the central characters' sexual mishaps and social humiliations in later life. In *American Pie 2* (Rogers, 2001) the old high school crowd are reunited as Jim and his buddies organise a predictably libido-fuelled (and misfortune-laden) party at a summer beach house. *American Wedding* (Dylan, 2003) sees Jim propose to long-term love interest Michelle Flaherty (Alyson Hannigan); Jim entrusting the wedding arrangements to the Stifmeister, with inevitably cringe-making consequences. And, nearly ten years later, *American Reunion* (Hurwitz and Schlossberg, 2012) finds Jim and Michelle struggling with the drudgery of parenthood and attempting to re-ignite their relationship at a high school reunion – an occasion for the original gang to reminisce about (and get ill-fated inspiration from) the hormonal escapades of their youth. Overall, the film franchise was a major box office winner, grossing close to $1 billion worldwide.

It was a success that also spawned a series of direct-to-DVD spin-off films. The first, *American Pie Presents: Band Camp* (Rash, 2005), sold more than a million copies in its first week of release, and three sequels duly followed – *American Pie Presents: The Naked Mile* (Nussbaum, 2006), *American Pie Presents: Beta House* (Waller, 2007) and the finale, *American Pie Presents: The Book of Love* (Putch, 2009). And, as fans were hungry for even more, further helpings of *American Pie* came in the form of no less than three 'making of' documentaries. 2003 brought not only *American Pie: Beneath the Crust Vol. 1* but also *American Pie: Beneath the Crust Vol. 2* and *American Pie Revealed*, all directed by Dave and Scott McVeigh and bundled with various DVD releases of the theatrical movies.

American Pie and the vulgar teen comedy

American Pie and its progeny stand as consummate (and especially lucrative) examples of the wider genus of vulgar teen comedy.

Sometimes known as 'teen sex comedy' or 'teen gross-out comedy', it is a category of film that parades the bawdy misadventures of goofball teenagers. Largely aimed at young audiences, it is characterised by a brazenly over-the-top humour rooted in the salacious, the scatological and the squirmingly tasteless. In the roll-call of vulgar teen comedies, *American Pie* is a key entry, but it was hardly the first. Released in 1978, *National Lampoon's Animal House* (Landis) is usually credited as the godfather of teen gross-outs, and the 1980s were littered with similar fare, from *Porky's* (Clark, 1981) and *Screwballs* (Zielinski, 1983) to *Revenge of the Nerds* (Kanew, 1984) and *Bachelor Party* (Israel, 1984). The 1990s, however, were a lean decade for the vulgar teen comedy, and its numbers waned as part of a more general decline in US teen cinema. The success of *American Pie*, however, heralded a resurgence.

The significance of *American Pie* lies in the way it breathed new life into the vulgar teen comedy, revising and reconfiguring the format for a new millennium. Indeed, *American Pie*'s reinvigoration of the formula was so successful it spawned a new era of low-to-medium budget vulgar teen comedies that all pushed determinedly at the boundaries of taste. Stretching across two decades, the roster boasts (if that's the right word) such pictures as *Road Trip* (Philips, 2000), *Dude, Where's My Car?* (Leiner, 2000), *Whipped* (Cohen, 2000), *Old School* (Philips, 2003), *Barely Legal* (Evans, 2003), *EuroTrip* (Schaffer, 2004), *Dirty Deeds* (Kendall, 2005), *Superbad* (Mottola, 2007), *Sex Drive* (Anders, 2008), *Mardi Gras: Spring Break* (Dornfeld, 2011) and *Project X* (Nourizadeh, 2012).

Whether the vulgar teen comedy represents a distinct film genre, however, is moot. Indeed, general debate surrounds how far, and in what ways, the concept of genre is applicable to 'teen cinema' or 'youth films' as a whole. Generally, scholars have viewed film genres as groupings of films that are distinguished by a common iconography – similar images, locations, historical contexts and so on. Alternatively, genres are seen as collections of films that share a similar narrative structure or a common set of visual codes and conventions.[5] For some writers, however, 'youth films' cannot be classed as a distinct genre. Instead, they are distinguished by their commercial imperatives – that is to say, they are marked out mainly by the kind of audience they are aimed at. Thomas Doherty (2002), for example, chronicles the rise of the 'teenpic', a variety of movie that spanned a number of film genres, but which was essentially characterised by its appeal to the newly affluent teenage audience of the 1950s. And, in a similar fashion, Catherine Driscoll also sees the 'teen film' as being 'determined most of all by its audience' (2011: 1).

At the same time, however, Driscoll acknowledges the way such movies are also often distinguished by recognisable 'generic' conventions:

> ...the youthfulness of central characters; content usually centred on young heterosexuality, frequently with a romance plot; intense age based relationships and conflict either within those relationships or with an older generation; the institutional management of adolescence by families, schools, and other institutions; and coming-of-age plots focused on motifs like virginity, graduation, and the makeover.
>
> (Driscoll, 2011: 2)

In contrast, Timothy Shary opts for a more simple, straightforward approach. For Shary, 'youth cinema' represents a distinct film genre comprising movies 'that are made about young adults' (2014: 20), though Shary argues this category, itself, encompasses a variety of distinctive subgenres – for example, the 'youth horror film' and the 'youth romance'.

American Pie and other vulgar teen comedies fit rather awkwardly among all these definitions. Certainly, they have been partly defined by their target audience. But, while teen cinemagoers certainly constituted their commercial base during the 1980s, by the 2000s such films were characterised by a strong cross-generational appeal. And, while many vulgar teen comedies *were* 'made about young adults', others also featured adults as central characters. Indeed, by the 2000s, films like *American Reunion* featured a cast full of adults, but still bore the familiar trademarks of the vulgar teen comedy. Moreover, *American Pie* and similar movies do not fit easily within Shary's generic classification of 'youth cinema'. In Shary's typology, *American Pie* is categorised as a 'youth romance', but it seems to sit rather uncomfortably alongside the likes of *Dirty Dancing* (Ardolino, 1987) and *Titanic* (Cameron, 1997).

Complicating matters further, Amanda Klein discusses the difference between the film *genre* and the film *cycle*. Drawing on the ideas of Rick Altman (1999), Klein argues that film genres are distinguished by the repetition of key images and themes, whereas film cycles are characterised by the *way* specific themes are pitched to audiences in a particular historical context (Klein, 2011: 11–20). As Steve Neale puts it, film cycles are 'groups of films made within a specific and limited time-span, and founded, for the most part, on the characteristics of individual commercial success' (2000: 9). Thus, while a *genre* provides an enduring blueprint for a collection of films across an extended time period, a *cycle* is more short-lived and taps into passing trends, often imitating the style of a single, especially successful movie. And the vulgar teen comedy could certainly be seen in these terms, having enjoyed two distinctive bursts of popularity – the first, during the early 1980s, followed the breakout success of *National Lampoon's Animal House* and *Porky's*, while the second, during the early 2000s, followed on the heels of *American Pie*. At the same time, however, it could be argued that the sheer endurance of the vulgar teen comedy amounts to more than a 'cyclic' popularity and, over time, its traits and characteristics have evolved into a discernible set of 'generic' attributes.

But academic debates about the intricacies of film genre invariably generate more heat than light. Overall, perhaps the vulgar teen comedy can best be described as a distinct sub-genre within the broad category of 'youth film', a sub-genre, moreover, that has enjoyed cycles of commercial success at specific historical moments.

Nevertheless, despite being both prolific and hugely popular, this is a collection of films that critics have invariably reviled as cinema's infantile nadir. The traditional view of vulgar teen comedy is that it represents, as writer Danny Leigh puts it, 'dim-bulb fodder for the young and easily amused' (Leigh, 1999). Moreover, it is an opus largely overlooked by film scholars. Even those relatively few texts charting the history and character of 'youth cinema' furnish scant attention on the vulgar teen comedy – invariably affording the movies just a nod of unenthusiastic acknowledgement, or a few grudging paragraphs of discussion. This book is the first concerted attempt to redress the oversight. While chiefly focusing on the original *American Pie* movie, it also considers the development of the *Pie* franchise as a whole, including the three sequels and four direct-to-DVD releases. But, as broader context, the book also charts the history, nature and appeal of vulgar teen comedy as a whole – a category of film that deserves to be more fully acknowledged in the history of modern cinema.

Before proceeding to deeper analysis, the book begins with an account of *American Pie*'s commercial development and a thorough outline of the film's narrative. Attention then shifts to the place of *American Pie* in the history of Hollywood teen films. *American Pie* is contextualised in the development of youth-oriented filmmaking, and consideration is given to the nexus of economic and institutional relationships that underpinned its production and box office success. Next, analysis focuses on the distinctive character of *American Pie* and other vulgar teen comedies, particularly the 'carnivalesque' qualities of their gross-out humour and the profoundly ambivalent place of women within these comedic strategies. Discussion then moves to the various ways 'youth' is configured in the *American Pie* series.

Here, attention is given to the way the original film marked a shift in Hollywood 'coming-of-age' movies, not only in its more explicit treatment of teen sexuality but also in its greater emphasis on dimensions of empathy and emotional transition. Close attention is also given to configurations of class and ethnicity in the *American Pie* series, and while the *Pie* franchise maintains the white, middle-class bias endemic to US teen movies, recognition is given to the place of the *Pie* films in a significant reconfiguration of portrayals of Jewishness in contemporary cinema. Particular time is also devoted to the analysis of *American Pie*'s configuration of young masculinity. There is close discussion of the *Pie* films' treatment of male friendship, and an analysis of the way the movies' representations of young men relate to broader shifts in social constructions of masculinity. Finally, the book highlights the 'nostalgic mood' of the *American Pie* movies and their melancholic portrayal of the transience and ephemerality youth – a quality they share with so many other entries in the broad category of 'youth film'.

Except…that's not quite it. Like the 'post-credit' sequences so common in contemporary movies, this book ultimately ends with a brief epilogue. Here, readers will find a discussion of recent trends in the history of the vulgar teen comedy. Especially highlighted is the impact of shifting attitudes to gender and sexuality, and the way a new crop of vulgar teen comedies has both reflected and been constituent in these changes.

Notes

1 For the unversed, 'hummer' is a slang term for an act of fellatio in which the person performing the act vibrates their mouth by humming, thereby intensifying the sexual experience.
2 See the DVD documentary *American Pie Revealed* (McVeigh and McVeigh, 2003).
3 The 'scientific' basis of this survey is obviously dubious. But, for curious readers, the poll's top spot was scooped by *Airplane!* (Zucker, Abrahams and Zucker, 1980), with an estimated three laughs per minute.
4 Unless otherwise stated, all data for movie budgets and box office returns are taken from the website *Box Office Mojo* (www.boxofficemojo.com/).
5 An accessible introduction to theories of film genre exists in Grant (2007).

2   A recipe for success

The rise of *American Pie*

Ingredients for a hit teen movie

The success of a movie is always indebted to a confluence of factors. Contextual forces are always important – for example, changes in the structure of the film industry and shifts in market demand. But also crucial are the qualities of the movie itself and the talents of the various people contributing to its production. With this in mind, this chapter details the development of *American Pie* and provides a thorough outline of the film itself. A close account is given of *American Pie*'s storyline to convey a flavour of the movie's take on the oeuvre of vulgar teen comedy. But it also serves to provide a sense of the film's overriding themes and will acquaint readers with *American Pie*'s main characters, their personalities and relationships. Attention is also given to the contributions of key production staff. Here, the important role of young producers Warren Zide and Craig Perry is highlighted, together with the directorial talents of the equally youthful Paul and Chris Weitz. And particular recognition is given to the part played by *American Pie*'s young creator, Adam Herz, whose own tastes and life experiences were the picture's inspiration.

Untitled teenage sex comedy...which readers will most likely hate but we think you will love

The son of a successful neurosurgeon, Adam Herz was born in 1972 and grew up in the upper middle-class environs of East Grand Rapids, a small, lakeside city nestling among the Michigan hills. From an early age, Herz had wanted to work in the film business and, using his mother's Super 8 camera, made his first movies while a teen. Clean-cut and bespectacled, Herz attended East Grand Rapids High School, where the former Assistant Principal remembers him as a 'shy, nerdy, nice little guy'.[1] Graduation in 1991 saw a move to the University of Michigan, where Herz studied film. The university, Herz has recalled, 'didn't have a strong production programme'.[2] Instead, he remembers, 'You studied movies, analysed and wrote about them'. One class would prove especially prescient. Titled 'Gross-Out Cinema', it combined the study of horror films and gross-out comedies, including *Porky's*, the vulgar teen comedy hit of 1981. 'I was a film scholar. I was a film student', Herz recollects, and, focusing on *Porky's*, he wrote one of his university papers on 'the use of space imparting guilt to the viewer'. According to Herz, the essay dealt with 'subjective camera stuff', adding with a grin, 'but it's such bullshit'. Nevertheless, his appetite for filmmaking was firmly whetted by a three-week internship at the New Line Cinema movie studio, where he worked on the teen comedy *House Party 3* (Meza, 1994), and after completing his studies, Herz headed out to Hollywood in 1996.

While working in a string of production assistant jobs, Herz began writing 'speculation' or 'spec' scripts – sample scripts that serve as a 'calling card' circulated to agents and producers as examples of a writer's talent. Penning spec scripts for the TV sitcoms *Seinfeld* and *The Larry Sanders Show*, Herz struck lucky when they caught the eye of Chris Bender, a manager working for Warren Zide and Craig Perry's production company, Zide-Perry Entertainment. As Bender recalls, the thing that struck him most about Herz's spec script for *Seinfeld* was that, 'there was a whole storyline about "golden showers" [laughs]. So that showed me a little bit of what Adam was capable of'.[3]

Producers Warren Zide and Craig Perry were also impressed. Both were young guns in the film business. Aged 28, Zide had founded his Los Angeles management firm in 1994, partnering with Perry in 1997. The pair mainly managed screenwriters, but they had also scored a recent success producing the action/comedy movie *The Big Hit* (Wong, 1998) featuring Mark Walberg and Antonio Sabàto Jr. Seeing big potential in Herz's work, Zide and Perry swiftly signed up the fledgling writer and began working towards a new movie. Recollections differ, however, as to who first proposed a teen comedy. Warren Zide recalls that he and Perry had been kicking the idea around for a while, though Herz remembers that it was he who put it to the producers that he had 'always had the idea to resurrect movies like *Porky's* and *Bachelor Party*'.[4] But, whoever's idea it was, Herz was duly tasked with writing a script that could reinvent the teen comedy.

Inspired by both his love of comedy and the misadventures of his high school friends, Herz finished the initial draft in a matter of weeks, writing some parts while on a ski vacation with his parents. But, while promising, the initial product was considered far too risqué. As Zide recalls, 'If anyone saw the very, very first draft, it would absolutely have been an "X" rating' (quoted in Parish, 2000: 113). But, eight drafts later, the script was considered ready to be pitched to prospective movie studios. Zide, however, anticipated problems with studio screenplay readers, whose job is to read submitted scripts and pass on recommendations to the studio executives. 'I knew the readers would hate it because it wasn't an art-house movie', Zide explains, 'and I had to come up with a clever way of presenting it'. So, after protracted brainstorming, the script was finally submitted with a title that was somewhat ungainly, but certainly attention-grabbing – *Untitled Teenage Sex Comedy That Can Be Made for Under 10 Million Dollars Which Readers Will Most Likely Hate But We Think You Will Love.*[5]

Much to the excitement (and pleasant surprise) of the young filmmakers, a bidding-war quickly ensued as three different studios clamoured to get their hands on the project. Ultimately, Universal was the victor, and paid out $650,000 to secure an option on the script. It was an extraordinary amount for a young writer's first screenplay, and Herz has recalled his astonishment on hearing the news in a phone-call from Zide:

> I was, like, 'Are you kidding me? Are you *fucking kidding me*?! Whaaat?!'.[6]

Getting set for great falls

Happy with their acquisition, Universal paid out a further $100,000 to swing the film into production. Clearly, the first thing the movie needed was a more workable title. On the submitted script, the addendum 'a.k.a *East Grand Rapids High*' had originally appeared beneath the more verbose moniker, and this addition was initially adopted as the film's title. The name was a nod to Adam Herz's *alma mater* in Michigan, but it made Universal's legal department very nervous. So, to avert a possible welter of lawsuits from outraged locals, the name of the film's high school setting was changed to East Great Falls High School, and the title of the movie itself was changed to *East Great Falls High*, then shortened to simply *Great Falls*. The studio also upped the film's budget to $11 million (Parish, 2000: 117). But, while this was $1 million more than the original script had envisaged, it was still decidedly low-cost by Hollywood's standards.

The search then began for a suitable director. The project needed someone hip enough to relate to the film's subject-matter, but whose fee would not dent the movie's finances. Universal initially considered hiring someone who had helmed successful music videos, which had become a common training ground for first-time feature film directors. Attention, however, soon switched to 32-year-old Paul Weitz and his 29-year-old brother, Chris.

Paul Weitz had been an aspiring playwright, while Chris had worked as a reporter and had been accepted for a post in the U.S. State Department. But the brothers' family had worked in the movie business for three generations, and the pair decided to try their luck at scriptwriting. Their collaboration produced *Karma Cop* – a screenplay about a tough New York cop who cracks cases by working with a nonviolent Hindu detective. It was a corny premise, but the screenplay sold.[7] This, together with a few other entrées into movie scriptwriting, allowed the brothers to progress to writing the screenplay for DreamWorks' hit computer-animated feature *Antz* (Darnell and Johnson, 1998). The experience gave them solid industry credentials, but, as comparative rookies, they were also cheap. It was a combination that made the Weitz brothers ideal for *Great Falls*, and in April 1998, they were signed up for their directorial debut (Parish, 2000: 115). Officially, the film credits listed Paul as director and Chris as a producer, though in practice the two roles blended into one. And, as the movie came together, Warren Zide and Craig Perry (together with their associate Chris Moore) remained hands-on producers. Staying close to the project, they provided critical input as well as keeping production on track.

In casting *Great Falls* the directors and producers looked for actors who could give a sense of veracity to a depiction of modern high school seniors. As the Weitz brothers later explained, 'We were looking for good young actors who could play well off each other... We checked out fifty to sixty actors at a time, and looked for chemistry between the couples' (117). The part of Jim Levenstein, the movie's hapless central character, was given to the fresh-faced, boy-next-door actor Jason Biggs. The 20-year-old Biggs had appeared in a variety of stage roles and TV series, but had limited experience in movies. The rest of the cast, too, were relative newcomers. The strategy was deliberate. With a cast that was virtually unknown, it was felt, the movie would avoid alienating potential cinemagoers who might stay away if the film featured an established teen star they already disliked (177). And using new faces was, of course, another way of keeping the budget down.

With crew and cast in place, *Great Falls* began filming in July 1998. Shot on the soundstages of Universal Pictures and locations around Los Angeles, filming was finished in just thirty-eight days. Moreover, the careful attention to costs paid off, ensuring the picture was completed for around \$400,000 *less* than its \$11 million budget (126). And, as preparations for release got underway, the popularity of the movie's test screenings took some executives at Universal by surprise. As Alyson Hannigan (cast as the film's loveable band geek, Michelle Flaherty) later recalled, 'The results...were so high, it scored better than anything they'd done for so long...the score was something like 97 out of 100' (quoted in Coy, 2017). The only thing prompting uncertainty was the movie's title.

Great Falls would have been quite an effective title. It made allusion to the movie's high school setting, but also neatly referenced the egregious mishaps of the film's teen heroes. The test screenings, however, suggested an alternative might have greater appeal (Parish, 2000: 126). So, given the popularity of the film's 'apple pie incident' with test audiences, the movie was retitled *American Pie* – the name poached from Don McLean's folk-rock hit of 1971. With the new title in place, *American Pie* was ready for its official premier on July 7, 1999, at Universal's CityWalk (the studio's glitzy entertainment district in California).

American Pie

From the outset, *American Pie* makes clear its stock-in-trade is a delight in spectacularly bad taste, exhibited largely through the abjection of its young protagonists. The film opens with a pre-credit sequence that sees high school senior Jim Levenstein settling into a convivial evening of 'jerking off' to badly scrambled porn on cable TV. As grainy images flicker, Jim squints to make out the action ('Oh, that was a tit. That was a tit! Yes!'), and he quickly sets to, with the help of a grubby sports sock pulled over his manhood. Just as he finds his stride, however, his attentive mom (Molly Cheek) breezes into the bedroom for a goodnight kiss. Red-faced, Jim snatches up a large cushion to conceal his incriminating crotch and mumbles a feeble explanation ('There's this nature show that I'm trying to watch, but...er...the birds are all scrambled and...and...'). But, before he can switch channels, a female voice from the TV porn moans loudly and implores, 'Oh yes, baby. Ride me like a pony!' (see Figure 2.1).

While Kevin's mom freezes in disbelief, his genial but straitlaced dad (Eugene Levy) ambles in from the landing. Turning to her husband, Jim's aggrieved mom declares, 'I think he's tried to watch some *illegal channels* here'. Springing to his son's defence, Jim's dad is reassuring – 'Illegal channels? This is just bad reception, honey' – but

Figure 2.1 Jim (Jason Biggs) has a convivial evening interrupted by his mom
         (Molly Cheek).

he is cut short as a male voice from the fuzzy TV bellows, 'Spank my
hairy ass!'. Bewildered, Jim's dad tries to avert further indignity by
grasping the TV's remote control from his son. Inadvertently, however,
he also grabs away Jim's cushion. And, as Jim's dad stabs wildly at the
handset's buttons, Jim is left exposed – his face a study in agonized
embarrassment as he sits on the edge of the bed, with a large, upright
sports sock clearly protruding from his boxer shorts.

As the main titles roll, the film's theme song kicks in – 'Laid', a
jangly and upbeat (yet somehow wistful) guitar number by British
indie-rockers, James. And, as the next day begins, students are rolling
up to East Great Falls High School. Stoically putting the previous
night's debacle behind him, Jim meets up with his three best friends –
Chris 'Oz' Ostreicher, Kevin Myers and Paul Finch. A tall and good-
looking jock, Oz is laid-back and plays for the school lacrosse team,
but is only slightly more worldly than the others. Kevin comes across
as a charming smoothie and is dating long-term girlfriend Vicky (Tara
Reid), but their relationship is as yet unconsummated. Paul – usually
known by just his surname, 'Finch' – affects droll, mochaccino-drinking
sophistication. Finch wears sports jackets, reads *The Wall Street
Journal* before class and can crack jokes in Latin, but he seems irredeemably square. The four friends make an unlikely group, but they
share important things in common. In their different ways, they are
all somewhat nerdy and socially inept. And, frustratedly but most
emphatically, they are all virgins.

The fact is gleefully highlighted by the school braggart Steve Stifler. A legend in his own mind, Stifler dubs himself 'The Stifmeister', but he is arrogant, obnoxious and makes an art of prolific profanity. Greeting Jim and his friends, Stifler radiates his usual lack of charm as he extends an invitation to one of his legendarily wild *soirées* – 'Coming to the party, you fuckface?'. But the invitation is laced with Stifler's malevolent humour. With his characteristic laugh (a piercing, self-congratulatory cackle), the Stifmeister underscores the foursome's woeful lack of sexual experience:

> I got an idea about something new. How about you guys actually locate your dicks, remove the shrink-wrap and fucking use them! I'll see you guys tonight. I'll look for you in the 'no-fucking' section!

Retreating ruefully to their favourite diner, Dog Years, Jim and his friends reflect on their lack of sexual success and discuss their game plan for getting laid at Stifler's party. More naïve than the rest, Jim curiously asks, 'Guys, uh, what exactly does third base feel like?'.[8] Grins flash across knowing faces and, with a lascivious glint, Oz assures his friend that it feels 'Like warm apple pie'. 'Apple pie, huh?', Jim nods in quiet contemplation, 'McDonald's or handmade?'. The exchange is idle banter – but it will have fateful consequences.

Later, Stifler's party is in full swing. His divorced parents are away, and the grandiose house is buzzing. But Jim and his friends' attempts at scoring all end in dismal failure. Finch aims for 'a fashionably late entrance'...and misses the party altogether. Jim spies the gorgeous Nadia (Shannon Elizabeth), a Czechoslovakian exchange student, but his attempts at conversation fall lamentably flat. Oz hits on an older college girl; however, she is majoring in 'Post Modernist Feminist Thought' and is unimpressed with his oafish approach to seduction ('Suck me, Beautiful'). Her laughter is crushing, but she shows good-hearted maturity by offering Oz the advice that, with a girl, he should 'be sensitive to her feelings. Relationships are reciprocal'.

Kevin's luck shows more promise, as he and girlfriend Vicky retire to a bedroom. Kevin is making a solid play for 'third base', but the couple are interrupted as a lecherous Stifler piles into the room with a pretty girl in tow. Kevin and Vicky make their exit, but not before Kevin, unable to stall his apex of sexual arousal, surreptitiously 'shoots his load' into a half empty beer glass left on the nightstand. Left alone with his prey, the Stifmeister begins to limber-up for love ('Take it slow, and let the good times roll'). Nonchalantly, he picks up the abandoned glass

Figure 2.2 Stifler (Seann William Scott) nonchalantly swigs the 'pale ale'.

and takes a hearty gulp of the 'jizz-spiked' beer (see Figure 2.2). At first Stifler is confused. But understanding slowly dawns and his face contorts with nausea as he pukes explosively. The scene cuts to the bathroom where a prostrate Stifler is heaving. His head is buried deep in the toilet bowl as Jim and his buddies savour the vignette. 'Hey, Stifler', Kevin jokes, 'How's the pale ale?'. His triumph, however, is short-lived. Vicky is fed up with her boyfriend's self-absorbed attitude to their relationship, and Kevin is unceremoniously dumped.

Other guests, however, are having a better time. Gathered around an oil painting of the Stifmeister's absent mother – henceforth referred to as simply 'Stifler's Mom' – two boozed-up teens enthuse over her sexy good-looks (see Figure 2.3). 'Dude, that chick's a MILF!', observes one, explaining, 'M-I-L-F... Mom I'd Like to Fuck'. 'Yeah!', his friend slurs, 'MILF!'. And the two characters (described bluntly as '"MILF" Guys' in the film credits) drunkenly punch the air to brainless chants of 'MILF!, MILF!, MILF!' before one plunges his face into the portrait's ample cleavage.[9]

The next morning Jim, Kevin, Oz and Finch wake in Stifler's lounge, hung-over and dejected. Their mood worsens as they spot Chuck Sherman (Chris Owen) seeing off a nice-looking girl. Sherman is renown as a hopeless dork, but fondly imagines himself as 'The Shermanator' – a sexually adept incarnation of Arnold Schwarzenegger's invincible cyborg enshrined in the 1984 film hit, *The Terminator* (as Sherman earlier boasts to Jim, he is 'a sophisticated sex robot sent back through time to change the future for one lucky lady'). And, as the front door

Figure 2.3 'MILF!, MILF!, MILF!' – MILF Guy #2 (John Cho) plunges his
face into the ample cleavage of Stifler's Mom's portrait.

closes, Sherman saunters up to Jim's group, pulls a conceited grin and
crows, 'Fellas, say goodbye to Chuck Sherman the boy. I am now a man'.
Bathing in his success, Sherman rams the point home. 'We were doing
the wild thing *all* night', he brags, 'I'm exhausted'. Unbeknownst to the
others, Sherman's boasts are a sham. But, for Jim's gang, their igno-
miny now seems complete. They have been bested by none other than
the arch-dork. The Shermanator.

Despair then sets in. 'You know, we're all gonna go to college as virgins. You realize this, right?', Jim laments, offering a grim forecast –
'They probably have special dorms for people like us'. But all is not
lost. Energised by a new sense of resolve, Kevin hatches a plan. Pro-
posing a pact that 'We all get laid before graduation', Kevin insists the
goal is within their grasp as long as they work together as allies, giving
mutual support and encouragement. 'Separately, we are flawed and
vulnerable', Kevin explains, 'But together we are masters of our sexual
destiny'. And, in the film's soundtrack, a rousing orchestra strikes up
as Kevin's speech hits an inspirational crescendo – 'This is our day!
This is our time!'.

Galvanised by the pact, the boys swing into action with renewed
vigour. Graduation and prom night are just three weeks away and
time is precious. Each formulates a plan for success. Outwardly, Finch
seems relaxed and works on his golf game – but, behind the scenes,
he has paid Vicky's best friend, Jessica (Natasha Lyonne), $200 to
spread rumours of his stallion-like prowess. The strategy pays off, and

girls flock to Finch as his reputation soars. Things go awry, however, when Stifler is turned down for a prom date by one of Finch's admirers. Out for revenge, Stifler laces Finch's mochaccino with laxatives and dupes him into using the girls' restroom, whereupon Finch suffers tumultuous diarrhea. Emerging to torrents of laughter from a crowd of students (with a grinning Stifler to the fore), Finch is left humiliated, broken and without a date for the prom. In contrast, his friends make better headway.

Kevin immediately sets out to win back Vicky. His attempts, however, are all resolutely rebuffed. So, in desperation, Kevin seeks counsel from Jessica who – much to Kevin's chagrin – explains that his poor sexual skill has always left Vicky decidedly unsatiated. Looking for help, Kevin turns to his older brother Tom (an uncredited Casey Affleck), and insists that he wants to make Vicky happy, rather than simply take advantage of her. Persuaded of his little brother's sincerity, Tom passes on the secret of 'The Bible' – an arcane manual of sexual technique compiled, added to, and covertly handed down through successive generations of East Great Falls students. Kevin duly retrieves the dog-eared 'Bible' from its clandestine cubbyhole in the school library. And, pouring over its crammed pages of explanation, notes and diagrams, he carefully takes in its voluminous contents. Then, fortune suddenly smiles as Kevin seizes on a chance to make up with Vicky. Things go well and Kevin is soon drawing on his wealth of new-found knowledge, deploying 'The Tongue Tornado' to transport Vicky to dizzying heights of orgasm. Success is thereby assured, as the pair agree to hook-up at the post-prom party.

Oz, meanwhile, looks for a new sense of emotional depth. Attempts at watching flower-arranging shows on TV prove unfruitful, but then Oz realises he could shrug off his muscle-head reputation by joining the school's Jazz Choir. His friends are doubtful, but Oz assures them, 'I can work the sensitive angle here, fellas':

> It's just like that college chick told me. All that you gotta do is just ask 'em questions, and listen to what they have to say and shit.

As usual, Stifler is dismissive ('I don't know, man. That sounds like a lot of work'). But Oz turns out an expert at close harmonies and wins the attention of Heather (Mena Suvari), a pretty choir singer. Impressed by Oz and taken in by his pretension of sensitivity, Heather asks him for a prom date. But the plan falls apart when she hears Stifler and the lacrosse team laughing about 'the choir chick' and assumes Oz was in on the joke. Oz, however, is genuinely smitten. Desperate to regain

Heather's trust, he volunteers to join her as a lead vocalist in the choir. But their relationship is dealt another blow when Oz realizes his final lacrosse game for East Great Falls clashes with the state choir competition. Torn between the two, Oz ultimately proves his devotion by abandoning the lacrosse game and sprinting to the music auditorium, arriving just in time to perform a stunning duet with Heather – to rapturous applause from the audience.

By comparison, Jim's travails are the worst. An attempt at Internet dating leaves his in-box resolutely empty, and there follows a succession of spirit-sapping humiliations. First, his dad, the ever-affable Noah Levenstein, takes him in hand for 'a little father-son chat'. The move is well-intentioned but excruciating. Jim squirms with embarrassment as Levenstein senior attempts paternal support by presenting his son with a selection of cheesy porn mags ('Oh... *Shaved...* That's a publication I'm not familiar with', Noah mentions as a blithe aside) (see Figure 2.4). And the torture continues as Jim's dad proffers ham-fisted sexual advice ('Do you know what a *clit-or-is* is?'). Then, a few days later, there comes the infamous 'apple pie incident'.

Returning home, Jim slings down his bag and yells for his mom. But she is not around. Walking into the kitchen, he spies a fresh-baked pie on the counter. Next to it, a note reads 'Jimmy – Apple, you're [sic.] favorite. I'll be home late. Enjoy! Love Mom'. Jim takes in the pie's aroma. Then, in the film's soundtrack, sleazy porn movie music begins. Jim takes a moment of thought; he slides a finger into the pie, slowly moves it around, studies the consistency. We can see the gears in

Figure 2.4 Jim gets some paternal advice from his dad – 'Do you know what a clit-or-is is?'

his head start to turn, as he recalls Oz's 'third base' analogy. The scene then cuts to the house exterior where Noah Levenstein is getting out of his car, carrying his briefcase. Coming through the kitchen door, Jim's dad stops dead in his tracks. His face drops, aghast. The sight defies comprehension – Jim lies prone, face-down across the kitchen counter; his shorts are pulled down, his hips slowly grinding into the flattened pie. 'Jim?', his Dad exclaims. Horrified, Jim looks up and in desperation stammers, 'It's not what it looks like!'.

A quick cut then unveils a scenario best described in the movie's original script:

> Jim and his Dad sit in silence, opposite each other at the table. Jim stares into his lap, humiliated. Jim's dad is crushed. You've never seen such disappointment…but he's trying to keep his chin up for Jim's sake. In the middle of the table is the pie. It's decimated. Mushed up, ruined…violated.
>
> JIM'S DAD (fighting back tears): I guess…we'll just tell your mother…that we ate it all.[10] (see Figure 2.5)

Things now seem hopeless. But then a ray of light appears as the lovely Nadia, out of the blue, asks Jim if she can come to his house and study with him. All looks promising until Jim lets slip to an effusive Stifler that Nadia will be coming straight from ballet practice and will need to change clothes. 'Fuck me!', Stifler enthuses, 'There's gonna be an Eastern European chick naked *in your house!*'. Jim's friends are equally eager and, against his better judgement, Jim is persuaded to

Figure 2.5 'I guess…we'll just tell your mother…that we ate it all'.

set up a webcam in his room so they can watch Nadia stripping over the Internet. So, upon Nadia's arrival, Jim surreptitiously arranges the webcam and dashes across the street to join Kevin and Finch at Kevin's house. Across town, Stifler also tunes in. And, as Nadia begins to change, her online audience start to drool. Nadia then finds Jim's stash of porn magazines. Aroused, she (somewhat improbably) begins to 'pleasure herself' passionately, half-naked on Jim's bed. A riotous reaction ensues from Kevin and Finch, together with Stifler and his irksome younger brother Matt (Eli Marienthal), and Jim is persuaded to go back and seize the chance to seduce Nadia while the moment lasts.

Nadia is startled by Jim's sudden arrival, but she has taken a shine to him. With a seductive Czech accent she coquettishly chastises him – 'You are a bad boy, James' – and orders him to perform a striptease. And, as electro dance music begins to pump, Jim strips to his boxer shorts, jigs about ludicrously and attempts sexy repartee ('Oh yeah, I'm naughty. I'm naughty, baby'). Watching from afar, Jim's buddies begin to groan, but things are worse. Jim is unaware that he has inadvertently sent the webcam link to everyone on the school's email directory. Consequently, the vision of Jim dancing in his underwear flashes onto the computer screens of teens throughout town – including assorted groups of guys and girls, a rock band in a rehearsal studio and even the grinning Shermanator. And, as a sexy Nadia sits Jim next to her, the world looks on in excited anticipation. The tension steadily builds…until Jim's sexual enthusiasm climaxes with undue haste. En masse, the Internet audience howl disappointment. But all is not lost. A desperate Jim pleads for Nadia not to go and wins her round for a second attempt. Yet, as Nadia lowers her panties, it is too much and, again, a quivering Jim peaks prematurely. Nadia swiftly exits, Jim is reduced to a nervous wreck and the East Great Falls student body is left in paroxysms of mirth.

Returning to school the next day, Jim is a laughing stock. His despondency is all the worse for hearing the incident has spurred Nadia's host family to send her immediately back to Czechoslovakia. A conversation with Michelle Flaherty, however, offers hope. Michelle seems a confirmed nerd. Her life appears to revolve around playing the flute in the tedious school orchestra. And, breathlessly gushing 'One time, at band camp…' in an annoying, sing-song voice, she is forever reeling-off inane anecdotes from her band camp past ('One time, at band camp, we weren't supposed to have pillow fights, but we had a pillow fight, and it was *so* much fun'). Nevertheless, Michelle is pretty and likeable. And, more importantly, she appears to know nothing of Jim's webcam tragedy. So, with the desperation of a drowning man, Jim asks Michelle on a prom date – and she gleefully accepts.

Prom night finally arrives. The prom itself, however, is tacky and the lame band are derided by the students ('You suck!'). Nevertheless, aside from a dejected Finch, who turns up alone, all the guys now have dates. Yet their mood is subdued. Apart, that is, from a fulsome Kevin – who cockily suggests a 'status check' on the friends' pact. It is a bad move. Oz and Finch are disinterested, while a burnt-out Jim finally cracks, angrily snapping that he's, 'sick and tired of the bullshit pressure' – 'I've never even had sex, and already I can't stand it. *I hate sex!*'.

Gradually, however, spirits lift. The solitary Finch is joined by Jessica who, feeling guilty for taking his money, offers to dance with him and even presents Finch with a gleaming hipflask as a gift. Then, Chuck Sherman's earlier 'conquest' learns of his deceitful boasts. Fuming, she takes the stage microphone and lays bare his dishonesty, averring that Sherman confided in her that he had never had sex with anyone. 'Once', she reveals, 'he tried to screw a grapefruit. But that's all'. Disgraced, the Shermanator suffers a major malfunction and wets himself. With Sherman exposed as a fraud, it is as if order has been restored to the universe, and Jim's gang cheerily catches the bus to the huge post-prom party at Stifler's lakeside mansion.

Amid the party revelry, each of the four boys ultimately fulfills their pact through making no conscious effort. In an upstairs bedroom Kevin finally consummates his relationship with Vicky, and strikes 'fourth base' after declaring his love for her. Meanwhile, walking along the lakeside, an emotional Oz confesses the boys' pledge to Heather. She is wary, until Oz renounces the pact and declares, doe-eyed, that he has 'already won' just by being with her. Passionately embracing, they move naturally and fluidly into their first sexual experience. And Oz, abiding by his newfound sensitivity, never divulges their lovemaking.

In the meantime, Jim is sitting on a sofa, nodding-off to Michelle's interminable 'band camp' stories. As yet another tiresome tale seems to begin, however, Michelle suddenly reveals she is not the humdrum geek Jim had assumed. 'One time, at band camp...', she announces, 'I stuck a flute in my pussy!'. Jim splutters into his beer with astonishment – 'Excuse me??!'.

'What?', Michelle cheerily elaborates, 'You don't think I know how to get myself off?'. Then, with a winsome smile, she asks, 'So are we gonna screw now? 'Cos I'm getting kinda ansty?'. And, as she leads Jim upstairs, Michelle discloses she knew all along about his webcam mishaps and had only accepted the prom date because she figured Jim would be a 'sure thing'. Consequently, Jim finally gets to have calamity-free sex, though a dominant Michelle leads in the passionate fray. 'What's my name?!', she commands ferociously, 'Say my name, bitch!', as Jim whimpers, 'Oh, God...!'.

An abandoned Finch, meanwhile, wanders around the empty basement. Drifting into the games room, he comes across Stifler's Mom (Jennifer Coolidge). She is sitting alone, bored and sipping a drink. Finch is immediately struck by her stunning beauty, and attempts sophisticated flirtation. Initially, Stifler's Mom is diffident, but she offers Finch some of her scotch – 'Aged eighteen years, just how I like it' – and gradually warms to his efforts at suave witticism ('... So I said, "This is *very obviously* a Pierro della Francesca!!"'). 'Mmm...you're dead', Stifler's Mom finally growls, grabbing Finch and proceeding to the billiards-table, where the two are soon exchanging hot-blooded ardour:

STIFLER'S MOM: I had no idea you'd be this good.
FINCH: Neither did I.
STIFLER'S MOM: Oh, Finchy. Finch!
FINCH: Oh, Stifler's Mom!

But, as *American Pie* approaches its conclusion, the party aftermath is decidedly bitter-sweet. Kevin and Vicky are in love, but neither seem happy and agree to split knowing that, after they have gone to different universities, the physical distance will make things impossible. Kevin is sad, but reconciled. Meanwhile, as dawn breaks, Jim wakes up in bed and rolls over to cuddle Michelle, only to find himself hugging an inflatable toy shark. Michelle has clearly deserted him. Thinking for a second, realisation dawns. 'Oh my God', Jim muses, 'She used me. I was *used*'. But he shrugs in happy resignation. 'I was used', he smiles to himself, 'Cool!'.

Finally, a very hung-over Stifmeister moseys into the games room. The vista of his mother in amorous embrace with Finch, however, is too much for him to believe. 'Mom??!', Stifler exclaims, before fainting to the floor.

Later in the morning, Jim, Kevin, Oz and Finch reconvene at Dog Years for breakfast. But, rather than boastfully celebrating the completion of their pact, the friends are thoughtful and reflective. The mood has a definite melancholic edge, but the boys are happy and hopeful, and raise their sodas in a toast 'To the next step...' as they prepare to leave high school and move on to university.

Then comes one last comedic coda. The film cuts to Jim setting up a webcam in his bedroom once again, then stripping to his boxer shorts and cavorting foolishly to a bubbly pop soundtrack. Watching at the other end, in Czechoslovakia, Nadia is smiling and laughing. Behind Jim his dad walks in, but Jim is oblivious. Noah Levenstein is momentarily stunned, but this time he sees the funny side of things. And the movie closes as Jim's dad dances out of the bedroom and shimmies across the landing, calling friskily to his wife – 'Sweetheart?'.

American Pie, then, represents a particularly well-crafted example of the vulgar teen comedy. Its success was indebted – at least partly – to the skills of its creators and production team, who delivered a movie that was well scripted, sharply acted and deftly directed and edited. But the movie's success was also rooted in its economic and institutional context. To understand these issues, *American Pie* needs to be located in the historical development of Hollywood's attempts to target a youth audience. This is an area explored in the following chapter.

Notes

1 The teacher, Sheila Pantlind, is interviewed in the documentary feature, *American Pie Revealed* (dirs. Dave McVeigh and Scott McVeigh, 2003).
2 See *American Pie Revealed*.
3 See *American Pie Revealed*.
4 See *American Pie Revealed*.
5 See *American Pie Revealed*.
6 See *American Pie Revealed*.
7 Nevertheless, perhaps unsurprisingly, *Karma Cop* never entered production.
8 For the uninitiated, the phrase 'third base' derives from the lexicon of American adolescence wherein a baseball metaphor is employed for progressive sexual milestones. While the precise attributes can vary, 'first base' normally signifies kissing, or French-kissing. 'Second base' usually refers to more erotic physical contact – groping, fingering and possibly 'hand-jobs'. 'Third base' sees things taken further and typically denotes oral sex performed on a guy or girl. 'Fourth base', meanwhile, represents 'doing the deed'.
9 The term 'MILF' was first coined during the early 1990s, but *American Pie* did much to establish the acronym within the modern sexual glossary.
10 The scene's script, together with a clip of the scene itself, can be found online at 'Script to Screen: *American Pie*', part of Scott Myers' *Go Into the History* website (https://gointothestory.blcklst.com/script-to-screen-american-pie-20c97cf1fba4). The scene was, in fact, shot in several different versions. *American Pie*'s original theatrical release featured a tamer incarnation in which Jim is seated in the kitchen, with the pie pushed up against his crotch. The more lewd version – with Jim humping the pastry on the kitchen counter – was instituted in the film's first (unrated) home video/DVD release in December 1999.

3 Getting a gross from gross-out

Hollywood, the youth market and *American Pie*

'Another Way Station in the Collapse of American Taste'

On its release, *American Pie* won plaudits from at least some critics. Writing for *Arizona Republic*, for example, Bob Fenster opined that, 'most parents will be appalled by *American Pie*. But most teenagers will howl at its rowdy sexual antics' (Fenster, 1999). And, in *Rolling Stone*, Peter Travers struck a similar note, enthusing:

> With teen movies reaching a formulaic, play-it-safe low point...it's a kick to see *American Pie* bitch-slap those guardians of good taste who would suck the vulgar life out of movies... It's having the nerve to dare and the style to land jokes that counts.
>
> (Travers, 1999)

Others, however, were less enamoured of the picture. Writing for *The New Yorker*, for instance, David Denby was only half joking when he surmised that, 'cultural historians will no doubt record it as another way station in the collapse of American taste' (Denby, 1999). And, inevitably, some audiences will dislike *American Pie*. Indeed, its underlying theme, championing the values of 'respecting others and being true to yourself', can feel trite and hackneyed. Moreover, to modern-day eyes, some of its humour – that based around the boys' voyeurism in the 'Nadia webcam' scene, for instance – can seem misogynistic, and certainly a bit creepy. And, generally, some viewers will regard the film's jokes as puerile and bratty.

What such criticisms miss, however, is the way *American Pie* actually makes a virtue of its goofy immaturity. Wearing its adolescence on its sleeve, it is a film that deliberately savours its own silliness. More than this, however, the movie also boasts many fine qualities. The acting is polished, while the script is sharp and well-crafted. Skillfully directed and edited, the film's set-piece jokes are also marked by superb timing and execution. And, perhaps most of all, *American Pie* treats its characters with affection. Rather than being simply one-dimensional vehicles for the outrageous gags, its high school kids are generally well-rounded and genuinely likeable (even the Stifmeister).

These merits go some way towards explaining *American Pie*'s runaway success at the box office. Premiering in cinemas on 7 July 1999, the movie charted as America's Number One film in its opening weekend, garnering more than $18.7 million. And, while that figure is itself impressive, some observers speculate the movie's earnings should have been even higher given the many underage cinemagoers who snuck into the theatre after buying tickets to another film (Going, 2018). But, while much of *American Pie*'s success is rooted in its intrinsic qualities as a film, the picture's triumph also owed a significant debt to its institutional context and the way it adeptly surfed the wave of the film industry's developing production strategies. This chapter, therefore, reviews *American Pie*'s place in the history of Hollywood teen films, and considers the way a nexus of economic and institutional relationships influenced the production and success of this defining example of vulgar teen comedy. Attention is given to the market shifts and commercial tactics that underpinned the release of *American Pie*'s precursors during the 1980s, along with the new business approaches that propelled the *American Pie* film franchise into the vanguard of a teen movie revival during the early 2000s. But the chapter begins by placing *American Pie* in the context of a long tradition of youth-oriented filmmaking dominated by the 'exploitation' industry.

Before there was *Pie*: teenagers, 'Teenpics' and the rise of 'Youth Exploitation' films

Vulgar teen comedies such as *American Pie* can be located, as film historian Lesley Speed argues, in a long tradition of 'youth-targeted exploitation films' (Speed, 2010: 824). 'Exploitation film', however, is a slippery term. In a commercial sense, *all* films involve 'exploitation' since studios seek to generate as much profit as possible through their production. As a category circulating in film culture, however, the term has had more specific use. As Ernest Mathijs and Jamie Sexton explain, the term 'exploitation' has come to denote a type of cinema that 'existed on the fringes of the mainstream, dealing with themes and images that the mainstream would not tolerate and exploiting taboo topics as a key appeal' (Mathijs and Sexton, 2011: 153).

The original 'exploitation' movies, however, had little to do with youth. As Eric Schaefer expertly chronicles, the very first exploitation pictures appeared in America during the 1920s and 1930s. Lurking on the margins of the film industry, they were screened in seedy, flea-pit cinemas, and were akin to a gaudy sideshow, offering audiences an exhibition of the astonishing and the outrageous. As Schaefer explains, the 'exploitation' category embraced a variety of subgenres – nudist and burlesque films, sex hygiene films, drug films, vice films, exotic and atrocity films – but all shared a common preoccupation with 'some form of forbidden spectacle that served as their organizing sensibility' (Schaefer, 1999: 5). By the 1950s and 1960s the 'classic' forms of exploitation cinema charted by Schaefer had largely disappeared, but the foundations for the new 'youth-targeted exploitation films' alluded to by Speed were provided by an explosion in teenage spending power.

The growth of the American youth market during the 1950s and 1960s was partly a consequence of demographic trends. Wartime increases in the birth rate, followed by the postwar 'Baby Boom' rocketed the US teen population from 10 to 15 million during the 1950s, eventually hitting a peak of 20 million by 1970. A postwar expansion of education, meanwhile, further accentuated the profile of youth as a distinct generational cohort (Modell, 1989: 225–6). The vital stimulus behind the growth of the youth market, however, was economic. A wartime rise in youth spending was sustained by a combination of part-time work and parental allowances, with some estimates suggesting that young Americans' average weekly income rose from just over $2 in 1944 to around $10 by 1958 (Macdonald, 1958: 60). It was hardly surprising, then, that commercial interests scrambled to stake a claim in the teenage goldmine. Of the $10 billion in discretionary income wielded by American youth in 1959, *Life* magazine estimated that 16% (roughly $1.5 billion) went to the entertainment industries as they eagerly chased the teenage dollar ('A New $10-Billion Power...' 1959). An obvious example was the rise of rock 'n' roll as a genre of popular music preeminently aimed at youth audiences. But the film industry, too, zeroed-in on young wallets.

As Thomas Doherty comprehensively shows, a new 'teenpic' industry was spawned as moviemakers developed concerted strategies to 'attract the one group with the requisite income, leisure, and gregariousness to sustain a theatrical business' (Doherty, 2002: 2). The new teenpics, Doherty argues, began with a wave of movies that capitalised on the 1950s rock 'n' roll boom, heralded by Columbia Pictures' release of *Rock Around the Clock* (Sears, 1956), a film Doherty regards as 'the first hugely successful film marketed to teenagers *to the pointed exclusion of their elders*' (57, original emphasis). But the teenpic was a diverse species, and Doherty identifies a wide variety of teenpic types, stretching from delinquency pictures such as MGM's *High School Confidential* (Arnold, 1958) and Warner's *Untamed Youth* (Koch, 1957) to syrupy romantic comedies (or 'clean teenpics') such as singer Pat Boone's pictures for 20th Century Fox, *Bernardine* and *April Love* (both Levin, 1957).

The rise of the teen market also fuelled a proliferation of drive-in cinemas. 'Ozoners' (as drive-ins were fondly known) had first appeared during the 1930s, but their numbers mushroomed during the 1950s. In 1946 the US boasted only 102 drive-in theatres, but by 1949 there were nearly 1,000 (Segrave, 2006: 37). Five years later there were more than 3,000, and in 1957 *Newsweek* hailed the drive-in as 'the biggest single development in the movie industry in years' ('The Colossal Drive-In' 1957: 86). While figures for overall cinema attendance declined during the 1950s, outdoor drive-in theatres positively thrived, so that by the end of the decade America's 4,700 drive-ins represented nearly a third of US cinemas and were accounting for over 24% of US box office revenues (Austin, 1985: 64, Table 1). A large part of the drive-in audience were young, suburban families, but, as Doherty argues, the youth market was also crucial, drive-in operators courting teenagers with open-air dance-floors, fixed-price-per-carload admission and special 'teen-targeted' late-night shows – which helped cement the drive-in's reputation as a 'passion pit' for amorous adolescents (Doherty, 2002: 91–2).

The explosion of teen spending was fundamental to the growth of the drive-in. But so, too, was the 'Paramount Decree' – a Supreme Court ruling in 1948 that ended the major studios' monopoly of American film distribution and exhibition.[1] The ruling forced the majors to divest themselves of their movie theatres, which was a boon to many independent drive-in theaters, whose access to big Hollywood productions had often been stymied by the majors. Additionally, the breakup of the major studios' monopoly gave a big boost to America's independent film studios. Deprived of their cash-cow movie theatres, the majors were forced to retrench and so were keen to rent studio space to independent filmmakers and even distribute their films. Moreover, as the major studios increasingly relied on the production of big budget 'blockbusters', their output of films fell. This created a significant gap in the market, especially among neighborhood cinemas and drive-ins who relied on double-bills and a quick turnover of featured pictures. As a consequence, independent studios eagerly stepped in to meet the new demand with an output aimed, to a large part, at the lucrative teen audience. Independent companies such as Marathon and Fairway International made bold plays for young cinemagoers, but it was always American International Pictures (AIP) who led the way.

Founded in 1954, AIP was the brainchild of Samuel Arkoff (a cigar-chewing business lawyer) and James H. Nicholson (a hotshot movie promotions man). Cashing-in on the new opportunities created by the changes in film distribution and exhibition, AIP was in the vanguard of a new wave of 'exploitation' studios whose pictures were churned out as quickly and cheaply as possible, were promoted with spectacular ballyhoo and – as Arkhoff explained in his memoirs – were targeted at the sensibilities of 'the gum-chewing, hamburger-munching adolescent dying to get out of the house on a Friday or Saturday night and yearning for a place to go' (Arkoff, 1997: 4).

AIP's 'youth exploitation' strategies, therefore, foreshadowed those that characterised the later vulgar teen comedies such as *American Pie*. Geared to teen-appeal, AIP films had break-neck production schedules and bargain-basement budgets where *every* expense was spared. As Arkoff later reflected, his hardnosed principle in filmmaking was always, 'Thou shalt not put too much money into any one picture' (1). AIP were also masters of the hard sell, with Jim Nicholson often coming up with a gripping movie title and a startling sales campaign long *before* any thought was given to a film's actual content (38–9).

AIP's output embraced the whole teenpic typology. Rock 'n' roll musicals were served up with *Shake, Rattle and Rock!* (Cahn, 1956) and *Daddy-O* (Place, 1958), while delinquency movies proved an AIP specialty, with the release of pictures such as *Reform School Girl* (Bernds, 1957) and *The Cool and the Crazy* (Whitney, 1958). And films such as *It Conquered The World* (Corman, 1956) and *I Was A Teenage Werewolf* (Fowler, 1957) tapped into teenage passions for sci-fi and horror. However, aside from light-hearted romps like *Invasion of the Saucer-Men* (Cahn, 1957) and *The Ghost of Dragstrip Hollow* (Hole, 1959), AIP's comedies were initially few. But this changed in 1963 with the release of *Beach Party* (Asher), a bubbly blend of music and gags that capitalised on the contemporary surfing fad. Starring pop heartthrob Frankie Avalon and Annette Funicello (a former Disney 'Mousketeer'), *Beach Party* was filmed in just two weeks for only $500,000, but proved a 'youth exploitation' hit, grossing $6 million and leading the way for thirteen more AIP beach movies. The humour of AIP's comedies, however, was a long way from the lewd and crude excesses of *American Pie*. The beach movies were all frothy, cheerful and full of innocent fun. It was only with steady changes in US movie censorship that the way was laid for the 'gross-out' aesthetic characteristic of vulgar teen comedy.

Fast times for teen cinema: the 1970s and 1980s

Introduced by the industry-sponsored Motion Picture Association of America (MPAA) in 1930, the Production Code (also known as the Hays Code after Will Hays, the first President of the MPAA) was a system of regulation that spelled out what was – and what was *not* – considered morally acceptable in US filmmaking. The code had been rigidly enforced, but by the mid-1960s it was proving increasingly difficult to implement. In 1968 it was finally abandoned and replaced by a new, more liberal, Ratings System that allowed for more explicit visual frontiers. Exploitation studios like AIP quickly seized upon the new possibilities, with a wave of movies characterised by greater levels of sex and violence.[2] But the major studios also quickly made the most of the greater leeway created by the relaxation of censorship. And, in so doing, the boundaries between the exploitation sector and the Hollywood mainstream became increasingly blurred. To be sure, since the 1950s, elements of exploitation cinema's predilection for shocking spectacle and hard-sell promotions had filtered into aspects of Hollywood filmmaking. But, as Paul Watson (1997) argues, during the 1970s the traditions of the exploitation industry were increasingly manifest in mainstream movies, with a greater enthusiasm for sensational content that pushed at the bounds of acceptability, together with an increased use of aggressive marketing. Indicative was *Jaws* (Spielberg), Universal Studios' shark-attack blockbuster of 1975, which combined the thrills and spills of oceanic carnage with an equally no-holds-barred promotional campaign.

The more relaxed approach to censorship also impacted on film comedy. Informed by the late 1960s counterculture, movies like 20th Century Fox's Korean War satire, *M*A*S*H* (Altman, 1970), courted controversy through elements of social and political critique. But the ribald excesses typical of 'gross-out' humour also began to surface in films such as *The Kentucky Fried Movie* (1977). Directed by John Landis and written by Jim Abrahams and brothers David and Jerry Zucker,[3] the picture is an anthology of sketches that parody many exploitation film genres, together with assorted TV commercials and programmes, news broadcasts and classroom educational films. The skits are deliberately crude and outrageous, and the film revels in its bad taste. In one sketch, for example, a news announcer tells the film's audience that the popcorn they are eating has been pissed in, while a spoof commercial promotes a company that has discovered ways to extract oil from acne, fast food and Italian people's hair (taken from combs in their trashcans) (see Figure 3.1). Turned down by the major

Figure 3.1 Extracting oil from acne in *The Kentucky Fried Movie* (1977).

studios, *The Kentucky Fried Movie* was independently produced by movie exhibitor Kim Jorgenson. But it proved a shrewd move. With a budget of just $600,000, the movie clocked up a worldwide box office gross of $20 million ('*The Kentucky Fried Movie*' 2019). The success clearly demonstrated the bankability of gross-out comedy. It was also a major boost to the career of Landis, who quickly secured the job of directing Universal's first foray into gross-out – *National Lampoon's Animal House*.

Released in 1978, *Animal House* can probably be regarded as the first *bone fide* vulgar teen comedy. The film was written by Harold Ramis, Douglas Kenney and Chris Miller who had been responsible for *The National Lampoon*, the most popular humour magazine on college campuses during the mid-1970s. Set in 1962, *Animal House* was inspired by the writers' college experiences and followed the misadventures of a slovenly fraternity house – Delta Tau Chi – and its battles with both the authoritarian Dean Wormer and a rival fraternity, the goody-goody Omega Theta Pi. Led by the madcap John 'Bluto' Blutarsky (John Belushi), the Deltas are relentless party animals and the movie follows their trail of wanton beer-guzzling and lascivious revelry (see Figures 3.2 and 3.3), escapades that climax with the students wreaking havoc on the college's annual homecoming parade. *Animal House*, therefore, did much to pioneer the trademarks of gross-out cinema, with a style of comedy rooted in riotous debauchery and gratuitous bad taste. Moreover, while it was released by a major studio – Universal – it bore all the characteristics that Thomas Doherty sees as the defining traits of the exploitation film – 'controversial content,

Figure 3.2 Party animals in *National Lampoon's Animal House* (1978) – Bluto (John Belushi) is emperor of the toga party.

Figure 3.3 Bluto offers naïve fraternity pledge, Flounder (Stephen Furst), advice for his time at university – 'Start drinking heavily'.

bare-bones budgets, and demographic targeting' (Doherty, 2002: 9). Indeed, *Animal House* was shot in just thirty-two days on a relatively modest budget of $2.8 million, and, with its college characters and gross-out humour, it was aimed squarely at the youth market. And, for Universal, appropriating the hallmarks of exploitation filmmaking proved a money-spinning strategy – *Animal House* earning a domestic gross of over $120 million.

During the 1980s, this kind of profitability underpinned an explosion of movies targeted at – and featuring – teenagers. But changes in film exhibition were also an important influence. According to Timothy Shary, the rise of multiplex movie theatres located in shopping malls was fundamental to the surge in teen films. As the heyday of the drive-in waned, the shopping mall emerged as a key site of teen congregation and provided Hollywood with a ready market of young consumers who, Shary argues, 'formed the first generation of multiplex moviegoers' (Shary, 2014: 7). And, for Shary, this was the moment that 'youth cinema' cohered into a distinct genre.

The face of 1980s teen cinema was provided by the 'Brat Pack' – a term coined by the press for a cohort of young actors who were seen as rising stars in Hollywood's new wave of youth films. Encompassing such figures as Emilio Estevez, Anthony Michael Hall, Andrew McCarthy, Judd Nelson, Ally Sheedy and Molly Ringwald, the Brat Pack were especially prominent in the school movies either written, produced or directed by John Hughes. Hughes' films were pivotal within 1980s teen cinema, Shary judging that 'no other director has so profoundly affected the way that young people are shown in films' (Shary, 2005:72). Hughes' pictures – most obviously, *Sixteen Candles* (Hughes, 1984), *The Breakfast Club* (Hughes, 1985) and *Pretty in Pink* (Deutch, 1986) – were not only box office hits but were also a major influence on the developing themes and style of teen cinema. Their appeal, according to film theorist Ann De Vaney, lay in their ability to formalise specific sets of visual and behavioural codes to denote different character types within the high school. These codes could then be transferred from film to film, Hughes deploying particular turns of phrase or items of clothing to evoke recurring character types. As De Vaney explains, 'A geek in a Hughes film…is usually recognizable by his large eyeglasses and mismatched clothes' (De Vaney, 2002: 203). The approach is exemplified by Hughes' most enduring school movie *The Breakfast Club*, which, as Shary argues, consolidated five key character types – the nerd, the delinquent, the rebel, the popular girl and the athlete – that not only recurred throughout Hughes' own films but also developed into lasting tropes of the high school movie more generally (Shary, 2014: 11).

Of all the subgenres of 1980s teen cinema, it was the horror film that offered, as Shary puts it, 'the biggest grosses (literally and figuratively)' (Shary, 2014: 9). The 'slasher' movie – wherein a deranged maniac stalks a group of feisty teens – proved especially successful. *Halloween* (Carpenter, 1978), *Friday the 13th* (Cunningham, 1980) and *A Nightmare on Elm Street* (Craven, 1984) were all huge box office hits and begat myriad sequels and imitators. But humour also did well. And, amid the 1980s boom in teen films, the trademarks of the vulgar teen comedy increasingly came together.

Fast Times at Ridgemont High (Heckerling, 1982) hinted at the shape of things to come. Chronicling a school year in the lives of a group of young friends, the film charts their social mishaps and sexual misadventures in two key subplots. The first sees Jeff Spicoli (Sean Penn), a goofball stoner – an archetype that became familiar in teen cinema – cross swords with his grouchy history teacher. The second subplot follows Brad (Judge Reinhold), a senior student who works crappy jobs to pay off his car and faces relationship strife with his girlfriend Lisa (Amanda Wyss). *Fast Times*, however, was something of a hybrid, drawing together elements of comedy, drama and romance. More squarely in the tradition of vulgar teen comedy were two Canadian films – *Meatballs* (Reitman, 1979) and *Porky's*.

Notable for actor Bill Murray's first film appearance in a starring role, *Meatballs* is reminiscent of *Animal House* in its portrayal of the madcap hi-jinks of counselors and campers at a shambolic summer camp, Camp Northstar. The head counselor Tripper Harrison (Murray) is a prank-pulling, girl-chasing fun-lover, and the movie charts his attempts to inflict chaos upon Camp Mohawk, Northstar's snooty rivals. *Porky's* humour was in a similar vein. Set in Florida in 1954, the film follows the antics of a group of high school teens set on losing their virginity at 'Porky's', a brothel in the Everglades. The redneck proprietor, however, cheats and humiliates the luckless lads, and the film charts their escapades as they seek revenge. Written and directed by Bob Clark, *Porky's* had been turned down by Hollywood's major studios, but was picked up by a Canadian company, Astral Films. It was made in the exploitation tradition – filmed quickly on a budget of just $4 million – but became a massive success, reaping over $109 million at the US box office ('*Porky's*', 2019).

In *Porky's* money-spinning wake, a sequel quickly followed, *Porky's II: The Next Day* (Clark, 1983), along with a growing flurry of vulgar teen comedies. In 1982 the independently produced *The Last American Virgin* (Davidson)[4] enjoyed moderate success, but it was eclipsed in 1983 by Geffen Films' *Risky Business* (Brickman), which grossed $63 million from its story of a high school senior (Tom Cruise) scoring illicit kicks while his parents are out of town. Independents and major studios alike followed suit, with a stream of low-budget, quickly made comedies centred on libido-driven teens, including *Spring Break* (Cunningham, 1983), *The First Turn On!* (Kaufman and Herz, 1983), *Screwballs* (Zielinski, 1983) and its sequel *Screwballs II: Loose Screws* (Zielinski, 1985), *Up the Creek* (Butler, 1984), *Hot Chili* (Sachs, 1985), *Fraternity Vacation* (Frawley, 1985), *Mischief* (Damski, 1985), *Hamburger: The Motion Picture* (Marvin, 1986) and *Hot Moves*

(Sotos, 1984) – the last being credited by Shary as the first movie to feature the archetypal plot of boys taking an oath to lose their virginity by a set deadline (Shary, 2014: 256). Particular success was enjoyed by 20th Century Fox, who did well with a string of teen-targeted gross-out comedies, including *Revenge of the Nerds, Revenge of the Nerds II* (Roth, 1987) and *Bachelor Party*, the last featuring a young Tom Hanks as dedicated party animal, Rick Gasko. And, of course, *Porky's* was also a key influence on *American Pie*, which breathed new life into the vulgar teen comedy after it saw a lengthy hiatus during the 1990s.

American Pie and the teen film renaissance

The lull in output of vulgar teen comedies during the 1990s was constituent in a more general downturn for US teen movies. While the 1980s were the heyday of teen cinema, Shary notes how the production of youth films declined considerably during the early 1990s (Shary, 1996: 158). Partly, this may have resulted from simple exhaustion, as both studios and audiences grew jaded with the relentless flow of teen pictures. In the case of vulgar teen comedy this may certainly hold true. As Adam Herz, *American Pie*'s screenwriter, explained in a 2003 interview:

> There was a lull in teen sex-comedies and sort of teen comedies in general because the genre killed itself. They started to really suck. They'd gotten everything they could and…there was like an eight-year span where Hollywood forgot that teenagers love movies.
>
> (quoted in Otto, 2003)

But demographics also played a part in the decline. As scholar and film market analyst Justin Wyatt observes, by the late 1980s the film-going audience was maturing, so that 'in 1990, the over-forty audience jumped 24%, while the under-twenty-one audience dropped 4% from the previous year' (Wyatt, 1994: 178). In response, Wyatt argues, Hollywood's output shifted. More films, he suggests, were targeted at older audiences, for instance, *The War of the Roses* (DeVito, 1989) and *Parenthood* (Howard, 1989). Others appealed to '*both* adults and their children', for example, *Home Alone* (Columbus, 1990) and *Look Who's Talking* (Heckerling, 1989) (ibid.). Leslie Speed also detects important shifts during this period, pointing to the rise of comedies such as *House Party* (Hudlin, 1990) and *House Party 2* (McHenry and Jackson, 1991), which 'developed an emphasis on intergenerational relationships', together with a cycle of goofy comedies that targeted multiple age groups and in which the categories of youth and adulthood often converged – for instance, *Bill and Ted's Excellent Adventure* (Herek, 1989), *Bill and Ted's Bogus Journey* (Hewitt, 1991), *Wayne's World* (Spheeris, 1992) and *Wayne's World 2* (Surjick, 1993), *Coneheads* (Barron, 1993) and *Airheads* (Lehmann, 1994) (Speed, 2018: 34–5).

While teen movie output declined during the 1990s, Frances Smith argues that the genre 'resurged at the end of the decade' (Smith, 2017: 15–6). This renaissance was, again, partly indebted to demographics and shifts in market demand. Although a long-term decline in birth rates continued, the youth populations of the US and many European countries had begun to grow by the end of the twentieth century as the 'echo' of the 'Baby Boom' worked its way through each nation's demographic profile. And, in the US, commentators talked of a new 'Baby Boomlet' as the children of the original 'Baby Boom' generation matured, and the number of American teenagers grew to 31.6 million by 2000, nearly 6% higher than the 'Baby Boomer' peak of 29.9 million in 1976 (US Bureau of Census, 2001). Youth spending power was also growing, market analysts Teenage Research Unlimited (TRU) calculating that between 1998 and 2001 the discretionary spending of the average American teen had increased from $78 a week to more than $104. As a consequence, TRU estimated that teen spending in the US had climbed from $122 billion a year in 1996 to $172 billion in 2002 (TRU, 2002). The prospect of this new surge in the youth market gripped many business sectors, not least in Hollywood, where the revival of teen spending power was at least partly responsible for Universal's determination to swing *American Pie* into production.

Other contextual factors, however, were also important. Especially significant was the runaway success of *There's Something About Mary*, the gross-out comedy hit of 1998. Written and directed by brothers Bobby and Peter Farrelly, the film recounts the attempts of Ted Stroehmann (Ben Stiller) to reunite with his old prom date Mary Jenson (Cameron Diaz), and is noted for two particularly outrageous scenes. The first sees Ted contorted in larger-than-life agony as he catches his manhood in his trousers' zipper; the second sees Ted caught with the gooey results of masturbation stuck to the side of his head, which his ladylove mistakes for hair gel and scoops away to sculpt her own fringe into a comically vertical peak. With a production budget of $23 million, the film had been a massive coup for 20th Century Fox, bringing in a domestic gross of over $176 million. The success certified the audience-appeal of gross-out comedy and Universal – keen to acquire its own gross-out hit – eagerly secured the rights to *American Pie*.[5]

Once in production, other contextual factors helped shape *American Pie*'s content. Censorship issues, in particular, weighed heavily on the film's development. In 1990 (and revised in 1996) the MPAA rating board had introduced the 'R' category, which allowed admittance to movie audiences aged under seventeen (providing they were accompanied by an adult). And, from the outset, *American Pie*'s creative team agreed that the film should push at the boundaries of taste and aim for an R rating, rather than the much more restrictive categories of 'PG' or 'PG-13'. As Herz, the movie's screenwriter, later explained:

> We wanted to show how teenagers really talk…Let's face it, high school kids are raunchy, and the funniest stories that come out of high school are the most appalling ones… To write a movie about sex and not have it be R-rated, you're not giving your audience enough credit. (quoted in Siegel, 2012)

At the same time, however, it was vital to avoid the much harsher 'NC-17' category. The NC-17 rating prevented admittance to anyone aged seventeen or under, which would clearly have been a disaster for a teen-oriented film. Moreover, many movie theatres refused to screen NC-17 films altogether, and many large video outlets refused to stock them. Understandably, then, Universal firmly cautioned Herz and *Pie* producers Warren Zide and Craig Perry to be very careful how they handled the film's most risqué scenes for fear of incurring the dreaded NC-17 rating.

So, in the lead up to the movie's completion, a protracted process of re-editing ensued as the *Pie* producers negotiated with the MPAA to ensure an R-rated release. The scene in which Steve Stifler swigs ejaculate-laced beer saw an early cut, with a dialogue reference to 'man chowder' duly deleted. The infamous 'apple pie incident' – wherein Jim Levenstein fornicates with a pastry desert – also attracted MPAA attention. As producer Zide later explained, 'We had to get rid of a few thrusts when he's having sex with the apple pie', as the MPAA asked, 'can he thrust two times instead of four?' (quoted in Nashway, 1999: 26). Nevertheless, in making their judgments, the MPAA were not entirely humourless. As *Pie*'s directors, the Weitz brothers, later recalled, '…as we were cutting things out, they [the MPAA] kept telling our post-production supervisor how much they were laughing at our material' (quoted in Parish, 2000: 127). In all, it took four return trips to the MPAA, but the theatrical release of *American Pie* was finally awarded its much-desired R rating.

Cranked out quickly on a minimal budget, and stretching the limits of taste, *American Pie*'s production was a throwback to the glory days of youth exploitation films. But the promotional stunts and hard-sell marketing surrounding *American Pie*'s release were also indicative of the way the practices of the exploitation industry had been absorbed into mainstream Hollywood. Months before the film's release, Universal's marketing office swung into action to create a buzz of anticipation. Advertising materials were pumped out to teen magazines, while the academic spring break saw a blitz of TV commercials on MTV. Adding to the pre-release ballyhoo, some risqué outtakes from the movie 'mysteriously appeared' on the Internet and were widely circulated. Meanwhile, in magazines and on *American Pie*'s official website, a promotional competition offered the lucky winner a 'rockin' end-of-the-school-year Summer Party', while runners-up received 'a party in your pants', winning a month's supply of condoms, ten Spankies and a copy of the *American Pie* soundtrack.[6]

Universal Pictures' executives, however, were divided over *American Pie*'s box office potential. The film had never been intended as a major release, but a few insiders realised it had the makings of a 'sleeper hit' and could be a surprise success. But others were doubtful, and, in an attempt to recoup some of the movie's budget, its foreign rights were sold off to the film distributors Summit Entertainment ('Universal May Have Egg…', 1999; 'Saying Bye-Bye…', 2000). It proved a costly move. *American Pie* earned an international gross of nearly $133 million, and in Germany it eclipsed *Mission: Impossible 2* (Woo, 2000) and *American Beauty* (Mendes, 1999) to become the most successful film of 2000 (Chartsurfer.de, 2019).

The extra helpings of *Pie*

Hot on the heels of *American Pie*'s success, a stream of emulators spewed forth (see Chapter 1). In the traditions of exploitation cinema, the new wave of vulgar teen comedies came thick and fast as filmmakers attempted to cash-in on the trend. Inevitably, the welter of movies that ensued was of variable quality, but some did good box office business. Two notable successes were 20th Century Fox's *Dude, Where's My Car?* and the independently produced *Road Trip*, both of which featured Seann William Scott (*Pie*'s Steve Stifler), who carved out something of a career niche in the genre. Other actors from the *American Pie* stable also featured in the new stream of vulgar teen comedies. For example, Shannon Elizabeth (*Pie*'s Nadia) became something of a sex-symbol and starred in the independently produced *Tomcats* (Poirier, 2001), while

Eddie Kaye Thomas (*Pie*'s Finch) featured in *Freddie Got Fingered* (Green, 2001). Jason Biggs (*Pie*'s hapless hero, Jim), meanwhile, went on to star in Columbia's *Saving Silverman* (Dugan, 2001), and was joined by Mena Suvari (*Pie*'s Heather) in *Loser* (2000), a teen comedy written, directed and co-produced by Amy Heckerling. Universal, however, did not get left behind. Eager to capitalise on their success with the first *American Pie* (and smarting from their misguided sale of the movie's foreign rights), the studio rushed a sequel into production.

Released in 2001, *American Pie 2* reunited the original's creative team, with Warren Zide, Craig Perry and Chris Moore producing the film, while the Weitz brothers and Adam Herz returned as exec- utive producers. This time the budget was upped to $30 million, and J.B. Rogers was signed up as director, while Herz supplied the screen- play from a story he had developed with David H. Steinberg. The orig- inal's ensemble cast also returned as, after a year away at college, Jim, Oz, Kevin and Finch meet up and – with the irrepressible Stifler in tow – spend a chaotic summer renting a beach house.

Amid the parties and gross-out shenanigans, several subplots unfold. Oz struggles to cope while his beloved Heather spends the summer abroad, and their attempts at phone sex result in a predictable mess. Kevin tries to figure out whether he can be platonic friends with his former girlfriend, Vicky. Jim, anticipating a possible reunion with the lovely Nadia, sneaks a trip to the notoriously geeky band camp to get tips on his sexual technique from his old prom date, Michelle. And, as she teaches him a few tricks, romance sparks and they finally become an item. Budding connoisseur Finch, meanwhile, yearns for a repeat assignation with Stifler's Mom and, in preparation, studies the sexual art of Tantra. Through its secrets, Finch claims, he has become a master of sexual discipline and can 'make an orgasm last for days'. When the object of his desire fails to show up, Finch is crest-fallen but accepts his fate. Yet disappointment dissipates at the end of the film when an expensive car pulls up to the beach house and Stifler's Mom rolls down the window. After a brief chat, Finch hops in and the car disappears down the road – much to the Stifmeister's chagrin. Another success, *American Pie 2* earned a domestic gross of over $145 million and laid the way for a third helping.

American Wedding was duly released in 2003. This time, Universal's confidence in the project saw the budget hiked to $55 million, while Chris Bender joined Zide, Perry and Moore as the credited producers and the Weitz bothers continued as executive producers. Herz also returned as screenwriter, and Jesse Dylan took up directorial duties. Since the last instalment love has blossomed between Jim and Michelle, and the film chronicles their mishap-laden wedding. Most of the original cast reprise their roles, and each features in the movie's various subplots. This time, however, it is Steve Stifler – clearly an audience favourite – who takes centre-stage, and the movie grandstands his outrageous antics. A key subplot pitches Stifler into competition with Finch for the affections of Michelle's little sister Cadence (January Jones), and the ensuing confusion sees a comedic role-reversal as Stifler tries to impress through the pretence of being a wholesome young man, while Finch takes on the persona of a foul-mouthed jackass. Losing out in the love stakes, Finch is alone and forlorn at the wedding reception, until Stifler's Mom arrives. Initially, they both agree they are over one another. But then Stifler's Mom invites Finch to her room – and the film concludes with the pair sharing torrid passion in the bathtub, secretly observed through the window by the awe-struck MILF Guys (John Cho and Justin Isfeld reprising their original cameo roles). *American Wedding* was less profitable than its immediate precursor, but still did respectable business, reaping a domestic gross of over $104 million.

The successive instalments of *American Pie* demonstrated the audience-appeal of both teen movies and gross-out humour at the beginning of the new millennium. But they also exemplified emerging business trends in a Hollywood that was increasingly relying on film sequels. As Michael Pokorny and his colleagues show, from the late 1990s America's major film studios responded to declining levels of cinema attendance by developing new strategies of risk management (Pokorny, Miskell and Sedgwick, 2019). Whereas Hollywood's principal mechanism for managing risk had formerly been to spread its film output across broad, diversified production portfolios, Pokorny et al. argue that studios have increasingly seen film sequels as a more reliable source of revenue than a diversity of releases. Drawing on the ideas of Derek Thompson (2017), Pokorny and his colleagues suggest that sequels are seen as an ideal way of producing films whose content meets the audience's desire for the 'optimally new' – that is to say, content that is perceived by the audience as being new and fresh, but is also reassuringly familiar and 'just like the products, ideas and stories they already know' (Thompson, 2017: 284). In these terms, film sequels and franchises have increasingly become the film industry's preferred method of generating 'optimally new' content, Pokorny et al. calculating that, between 1988 and 2015, the proportion of studio budgets spent on sequels grew from 10.5% to 25.9%, while the proportion of studio profits generated by sequels grew from 20.6% to 35.1% (Pokorny, Miskell and Sedgwick, 2019: 32). This reliance on 'optimally new' film sequels was exemplified in teen cinema. During the early

1980s franchises such as *Meatballs* and *Porky's* had already spawned a seemingly inexhaustible flow of follow-ups, and the trend was continued by *American Pie* and its various offspring.[7]

American Pie's 'afterlife' also epitomized broader industry trends. Subsequently released on video and DVD formats, *American Pie* was a clear demonstration of the way the film business was increasingly deriving new revenue streams from ancillary markets, so that by the mid-2000s a typical movie generated only around 20% of its total earnings from its theatrical release (Waterman, 2005: 66–7). And, alongside the video releases of the theatrical *Pie* movies, Universal Pictures found even more ways of wringing cash from the *American Pie* franchise.

During the late 1980s, while teen films lost their prominence at the cinema, Shary argues, their popularity was maintained through both the home video market and the release of cheap sequels to previous hits (Shary, 2014: 9). And, in the mid-2000s, Universal adopted a similar strategy when it released a series of direct-to-DVD movies bearing the 'American Pie' brand-mark. An increasingly common practice during the 2000s, direct-to-DVD films (as the name suggests) did not have a theatrical release, but were usually cheap, quickly made successors to box office winners and were released straight onto the DVD market. And, faced with *American Wedding*'s dip in earnings (compared to *American Pie 2*), it was a strategy Universal found attractive. Consequently, the studio chose to skip a further theatrical *Pie* release and, instead, extended the franchise through a succession of *American Pie Presents...* direct-to-DVD spin-off movies. The direct-to-DVD releases, however, had *much* lower production and marketing budgets than the theatrical releases, and the original creative team had little involvement. And, aside from Eugene Levy (who reprised his role as the ever-amiable Noah Levenstein), virtually none of the original cast appeared. Instead, fresh (and cheaper) faces were hired for a series of spin-off tales based on the exploits of Steve Stifler's extended family.

Released at the end of 2005, the first in the DVD series – *American Pie Presents: Band Camp* – sees Steve Stifler's younger brother, Matt, eager to carry on the Stifmeister's licentious legacy. Masterminding a disastrous school prank, however, lands him in serious trouble and he is banished to band camp. With a budget of under $15 million, the movie is lacklustre compared to its theatrical forerunners, but it turned a handsome profit for Universal, selling over a million units in its first week of release and ensuring a quick successor (Balchack, 2006). The following year, therefore, saw the production of *American Pie Presents: The Naked Mile*. This time Erik Stifler (John White) takes the spotlight. The cousin of Steve and Matt Stifler, Erik, struggles to live up to the family name and seems set to graduate from high school as a virgin. Salvation, however, arrives when his friends Cooze (Jake Siegel) and Ryan (Ross Thomas) take Erik on a road trip to visit his uproarious cousin, Dwight Stifler (Steve Talley), at college. Again, the film was made on a budget of around $15 million and was another commercial success, with sales of $27.5 million.[8]

The next instalments, however, were less auspicious. Released in 2007, *American Pie Presents: Beta House* saw the return of the previous film's writer and producer – Erik Lindsay and W.K. Border, respectively – together with four of the principal cast. This time, Erik Stifler and Cooze arrive as freshmen at the University of Michigan. Pledging to cousin Dwight's Beta House fraternity, the duo undertake a succession of 'gross-out' initiation rituals and then compete against the rival Geek fraternity (formed by wealthy nerds) in the Greek Olympiad – a series of challenges so outrageous they have been banned on campus for the last forty years. Even cheaper than its predecessors, *Beta House* had a budget of just $10 million, but its sales of around $18 million were also less impressive. And the decline continued with the last episode, 2009's *American Pie Presents: The Book of Love*. This time the movie sees a fresh generation of students at East Great Falls High School discover 'The Bible' – the arcane sex manual featured in the original film. Intervening years, however, have seen the sacred tome succumb to water damage and the kids set out to restore it to its former glory. *The Book of Love*, however, was probably the *Pie* nadir. Produced for just $7 million, the film scored barely more than $5 million in sales and was generally panned by reviewers. In response, Universal pulled the plug on the direct-to-DVD series and it looked as though the *American Pie* franchise had reached its end.

But, just as the direct-to-DVD series was ending, Universal Pictures announced plans for a fourth theatrically released *American Pie* movie. This time the film was written and directed by Jon Hurwitz and Hayden Schlossberg. Adam Herz, however, returned as a credited producer, along with the established team of Warren Zide, Craig Perry and Chris Moore. Completed in 2012, *American Reunion* saw the original cast reassembled as we catch up with the lives of *Pie*'s characters. Time has not been especially kind to them. Jim works in an office cubicle, while he and Michelle struggle with parenthood and search for ways to rekindle their sex life. Kevin is a home-working architect, but is browbeaten by his overbearing wife. Oz is a rich sportscaster living in Los Angeles with a supermodel girlfriend, but his life seems moribund. Finch tells his friends that he has been having exotic adventures traveling the world, but it soon transpires he actually works as an assistant manager in a stationery shop. A business-suited Stifler, meanwhile, is seen strolling into his workplace. Grinning broadly, he casually hits on women and cheerfully mocks his colleagues ('Morning, co-workers and cock-jerkers!'). Sauntering into an executive office, he puts his feet on the desk, grabs a framed photo of an attractive blonde and rubs it lasciviously against his crotch. Then, however, he is interrupted as his mean-spirited boss arrives, and it is revealed that the Stifmeister is actually just an office temp. Berated by the boss, Stifler is told to get back to work.

Things, however, perk up when, over ten years after their high school graduation, the gang return to East Great Falls for a weekend reunion. The familiar gross-out calamities ensue, but by the end of the movie, the characters are more contented with their lives and relationships. And, to maintain their friendship, they agree to meet up every year.

American Reunion, however, met with mixed box office results. At $50 million, it had a moderate budget, and its opening weekend saw it placed second in box office returns. Ultimately, however, its domestic gross was a disappointing $57 million. Nevertheless, this was offset by a buoyant international return, with a worldwide gross of over $234 million. The sales arithmetic exemplified the increased importance of foreign markets to Hollywood, Pokorny and his colleagues calculating that the contribution made by foreign markets to the major studios' revenues grew from 45% in 1988 to 61% in 2015 (Pokorny, Miskell and Sedgwick, 2019: 32). In view of this, possibilities remained for a further instalment in the *American Pie* saga – especially given the continued popularity of gross-out comedy.

Overall, then, the success of the *American Pie* franchise was constituent in wider shifts in Hollywood's business strategies. Growing from a long tradition of youth-oriented movies originally rooted in the exploitation film industry, *American Pie* exemplifies the way the style and marketing techniques of the exploitation sector increasingly impacted on more mainstream filmmaking. Moreover, *Pie*'s success at the end of the 1990s testifies to a wider resurgence of teen cinema as Hollywood sought to tap into a general revival of the US youth market during the late 1990s and early 2000s. *American Pie*, furthermore, exemplifies the way vulgar teen comedies were especially prominent in this renaissance, and the following chapter explores the nature, development and appeal of these movies' distinctive brand of 'gross-out' humour.

Notes

1 For a full account of the 'Paramount Decree' and its impact on the US film industry, see Tzioumakis (2006: 101–34).
2 The trend was exemplified by a crop of violent exploitation movies that capitalised on the contemporary notoriety of motorcycle gangs such as the Hells Angels.

3 The trio went on to write and direct the hit comedy movies *Airplane!* (1980) and *Top Secret!* (1984), together with the *Police Squad!* TV Series (ABC, 1982) and its film spin-offs – *The Naked Gun* (1988), *The Naked Gun 2½* (1991) and *The Naked Gun 33⅓* (1994).

4 Written and directed by Boaz Davidson, *The Last American Virgin* was effectively a remake of Davidson's 1978 Israeli film *Eskimo Limon* (*Lemon Popsicle*), which had enjoyed unexpected international success.

5 On its release *American Pie* capitalised on the success of the Farrelly brothers' movie, with a promotional tagline that mixed cheeky innuendo with an allusion to the earlier film – 'There's something about your first piece'.

6 They are probably best forgotten, but, at the time, Spankies were a proprietary brand of 'washable sleeve' designed to aid male masturbation.

7 *Meatballs* was followed by three sequels – *Meatballs Part II* (dir. Ken Wiederhorn, 1984), *Meatballs III: Summer Job* (dir. George Mendeluk, 1986) and *Meatballs 4: To the Rescue* (dir. Bob Logan, 1992). After *Porky's* there came *Porky's II: The Next Day* (dir. Bob Clark, 1983), *Porky's Revenge!* (dir. James Komack, 1985) and, later, a remake of the original titled *Porky's Pimpin' Pee Wee* (Brian Trenchard-Smith, 2009).

8 Financial data for the *American Pie Presents ...* direct-to-DVD series is taken from the website *The Numbers* (www.the-numbers.com).

4 'Like warm apple pie...'
Gross-out humour and the vulgar teen comedy

'Oh, Gross!'

Actor Jason Biggs has been rueful about the misfortunes of Jim Levenstein, the central character he plays in *American Pie*. 'Jim's life is one unbroken string of embarrassing moments', Biggs has acknowledged, 'Mortification. Utter mortification. Somehow, against what would seem impossible odds, he manages to play out every sexually humiliating experience of his life in full view of an audience' (quoted in Siegel, 2012). Adam Herz, screenwriter of the *American Pie* franchise, agrees. 'One constant in the series', Herz has reflected, 'has been the abuse of Jason Biggs's character and his genitalia.... Jim has to abuse his penis in every *Pie* movie' (quoted in Otto, 2003). The recurring theme of Jim's sexual disasters is complemented by *American Pie*'s enthusiasm for the scatological, the embarrassing and the perverse. Emblematic of the whole tradition of vulgar teen comedy, *American Pie* comprises a parade of set-piece gags that revolve around the rude, the crude and a delight in the transgression of acceptable taste. As such, *American Pie* and its ilk bear all the hallmarks of what has become known as 'gross-out' humour.

'Gross-out' films, as William Paul argues in his pioneering study of the oeuvre, are movies that celebrate 'gross physical existence'. For Paul, the vulgar comedies and bloodthirsty horror films of the 1970s and 1980s can both be considered 'gross-out' genres because – while one promotes laughter, and the other inspires terror – they share common ground insofar as they are both 'quite happy to present themselves to the public as spectacles of the worst possible taste' (Paul, 1994: 4). Gross-out movies, Paul argues, reverse normal priorities so that they not only embrace bad taste but also transform revulsion into a sought-after goal. The basis of their allure, therefore, lies in their dimensions of license and their determination to abandon all standards of decorum. As Paul explains:

> A gleeful uninhibitedness is certainly the most striking feature of these films – of *both* the comedies and the horror films – and it also represents their greatest appeal. At their best, these films offer a real sense of exhilaration, not without its disturbing quality, in testing how far they can go, how much they can show without making us turn away, how far they can push the boundaries to provoke a cry of 'Oh, gross!' as a sign of approval, an expression of disgust that is pleasurable to call out.
>
> (20)

American Pie exemplifies gross-out cinema's glee at pushing at the boundaries of taste. Like all vulgar teen comedies, *American Pie*'s humour is rooted in challenging normal standards of behaviour through explicit and excessive physicality. Its visual gags are preoccupied with bodily processes of ingestion and excretion, and its farcical set-pieces transform adolescent sexuality from embarrassed withdrawal into exuberant display. Jim's sexual experimentation with a freshly baked pie is, of course, a key example (see Figure 4.1) As he stands in the kitchen, sizing-up the dessert and clearly reflecting on his buddy's carnal analogy, the audience's feelings of distaste and disbelief are pushed to the maximum – is Jim *really* going to go that far? Is he *really* going to see if the sexual milestone of 'third base' *literally* feels 'like warm apple pie'? Surely not? Then, as Jim is discovered by his incredulous Dad, *in flagrante delicto* amid a heap of pastry detritus, the audience is left both squirming in empathetic shame and laughing delightedly at the outrageous spectacle.

Figure 4.1 Jim reflects on his buddy's analogy – 'like warm apple pie...'

The challenge gross-out aesthetics pose to prevailing standards of taste can be seen as related to wider social and political relationships. As the influential cultural theorist Pierre Bourdieu (1984) argues, rather than being neutral sets of intrinsic and inherent values, 'tastes...function as markers of "class"' (1984: 1–2). Tastes, Bourdieu contends, are intimately connected with hierarchies of status and authority. Those groups of greater wealth and 'higher' social class tend to cultivate a taste for subtlety and refinement as a way of demonstrating their possession of 'cultural capital' – that is to say, resources of knowledge and discrimination acquired through education and processes of socialisation. In these terms, 'refined' taste is less important in itself than as a way of distinguishing the members of some groups from others. Film theorist Geoff King (2002: 72) applies this to the context of film comedy by suggesting that those wishing to define themselves as being of 'superior' social standing are likely to reject forms of entertainment such as gross-out comedy, with its emphasis on corporeality and the transgression of bodily boundaries, in favour of supposedly more 'subtle' and cerebral comic formats.

In contrast, King argues, 'lower' forms of comedy – defined as 'crude' and lacking in subtlety – have usually been seen as the preserve of either the young or groups of lower social standing. Enjoyment of 'crude' entertainment, King explains, 'requires fewer reserves of expensively acquired cultural capital, and so is accessible to those of lesser means' (72). Moreover, such entertainment also offers 'more intense and immediate returns of pleasure, qualities seen by Bourdieu as appropriate to the needs of lower class audiences seeking short-term release from the rigours of their existence' (ibid.). In these terms, therefore, the wilful transgression of established standards of taste carries with it the potential for deeper challenges to social hierarchies. As a consequence, some theorists have imputed a subversive, even radical, dimension to elements of gross-out comedy.

This chapter considers *American Pie* in the context of such debates. It begins by charting the emergence and development of gross-out comedy through the 1950s, 1960s and 1970s, then critically considers the character of the vulgar teen comedies that proliferated during the 1980s. The specific cultural meanings and social significance of *American Pie* are then considered in depth. Particular attention is given to the film's 'carnivalesque' qualities and its propensity for transgression through outrageous spectacles and jaw-dropping displays of bad taste. The discussion concludes with an express focus on *American Pie*'s representation of women and a consideration of the movie's profoundly ambivalent – and relatively open-ended – sexual politics.

'Going Too Far': the rise of gross-out comedy

The roots of modern gross-out comedy are usually traced to America's 'sick' comedians of the late 1950s and early 1960s. The term 'sick humour' was applied to a new style of comedy associated with figures such as Lenny Bruce, Dick Gregory, Shelley Berman and Mort Sahl, whose comic style courted controversy through its elements of cynicism, social criticism and political satire. For William Paul, the abrasive attitude of these comics resonated, with the wider challenges being made to the social and political establishment by movements such as the campaign for civil rights and the fight for women's liberation. 'Through all these movements', Paul argues, 'there is an underlying intent to make the private public property, to bring out into the open "closeted" prejudices as a way to destroy them' (Paul, 1994: 45). In these terms, then, there was a political facet to sick comedy in the way its humour worked, like the radical movements of the time, to expose the hypocrisies and injustices many felt were at the heart of US society.

This rebellious brand of comedy, Paul argues, burgeoned during the 1960s as a consequence of two key factors. First, across cultural life, a series of successful battles against obscenity laws gradually rolled back systems of censorship, a move exemplified by the end of Hollywood's Production Code in 1968 (see Chapter 3). Second, the post-war Baby Boom and an expansion of college education created a prolific youth culture that was often characterised by a sense of revolt against established orthodoxies, and which provided a ready audience for subversive humour (38–45). The important role of youth culture is underscored by writer Tony Hendra, who coins the term 'Boomer humor' for what he sees as a form of comedy peculiar to the post-war Baby Boom generation. 'Boomer humor', Hendra argues, shared the seditious zeal that had characterised the 'sick' comedians of the 1950s. But, whereas 'sick comedy' challenged the status quo through the sharp edge of satire, 'Boomer humor' was more anarchic. Exuberant and over-the-top, 'Boomer humor' contested conservative tenets by flouting conventional morality and fervently defying accepted standards of taste. As Hendra puts it:

> Where classical satire expresses revulsion at the departure from widely held standards, Boomer humor seems to operate in the other direction, rejecting standards, searching for new ones, experimenting with limits, pushing taste and – more often than not – Going Too Far.

> (Hendra, 1987: 10)

'Boomer humor' flourished throughout the 1960s and 1970s. Indicative, Hendra argues, was the popularity of 'Boomer humor' comics
such as Richard Pryor and the Smothers Brothers, along with the
success of the magazine he edited from 1971 to 1978, *The National
Lampoon*. Launched in 1970, *The National Lampoon*'s mixture of ar-
ticles, cartoons and comic strips was a hit with young readers and its
circulation grew to a peak of over a million a month in 1974 (Hendra,
1987: 378). Combining intelligent, cutting-edge wit with gusto for the
crass and the bawdy, the magazine was – according to Hendra – 'the
apotheosis of Going Too Far' (Hendra, 1987: 20). Alongside its print
incarnation, the *Lampoon* also spawned a series of stage and radio
shows that premiered the talents of such comic luminaries as John
Belushi, Chevy Chase and Bill Murray. And, in 1978, the magazine's
creative flair was transferred to the silver screen with the release of
National Lampoon's Animal House.

With its fraternity food fights, riotous toga parties and assorted
sexual antics, *Animal House* marked the arrival of the vulgar teen
comedy. But, for many critics, the film was not simply an exercise in
ribald fun. Hendra, for example, argues that behind the tale of an
errant fraternity's struggle with despotic college authorities was a
'driving spirit of anarchy' (Hendra, 1987: 397) that carried forward
many of the major themes that had preoccupied 'Boomer humor' –
'Conformity, corruption at the top, the sanity of "insanity" versus psy-
chotic "normality", sexual freedom, abiding contempt for the military
and the lunacy it forces into everyday life...' (401). William Paul also
detects a defiant impulse in the movie, arguing that it was a progenitor
of a broader trend towards what he terms 'Animal Comedy', a style of
humour that fuses together gross-out vulgarity, a struggle for sexual
liberty and a generational challenge to dominant power structures:

> Much as Animal Comedy celebrates sexual liberation, it also cele-
> brates an antiauthoritarian social liberation. The authority figures
> in these films are inevitably repressive and almost as inevitably
> male. They are also inevitably adults trying to keep youngsters
> in line, so that the parent-child relationship is implicitly invoked.
>
> (Paul, 1994: 122)

A raw, oppositional attitude was hardly new in youth movies. Hitherto,
however, it had tended to reside on the margins of the film industry,
for example, in the twisted sneer of the delinquents that populated
AIP's 1950s exploitation pictures. *Animal House* marked its move into
the mainstream. As Paul explains, 'What is most striking about *Animal House* in the history of Hollywood comedy is not its vulgarity

but rather the vulgarity within the wrappings of slick and seemingly high production values' (92). Moreover, Paul argues, the huge commercial success of *Animal House* heralded a sea-change in the history of US film comedy (86). Since the 1920s, the boy-meets-girl blueprint of romantic comedies had dominated Hollywood's comic output, but, Paul contends, it was quickly eclipsed when the runaway popularity of *Animal House* prompted a veritable tsunami of vulgar teen movies – from *Porky's* and *Meatballs* to *Revenge of the Nerds* and *Bachelor Party* (see Chapter 3).

For some critics, however, the later vulgar teen comedies lacked the mutinous spirit of *Animal House*. 'Within a movie or two', Hendra argues, 'Hollywood had made the unique blend of anarchic skepticism of *Animal House* into a formula of conformist rebellion against unthreatening authority, converting its ebullience into the familiar dreary celebration of misogyny and titillation' (1987: 24).[1] Paul tends to agree. During the 1980s, Paul suggests, gross-out's elements of defiance were steadily defused as its aesthetics became blandly formulaic and its radical drive gave way to the attitude of smug, self-centred individualism so characteristic of the Reagan era (1994: 429–30). Indeed, after it became banal and conformist, gross-out entered a decline. Consequently, Paul argues, by the late 1980s the sedate conventions of romantic comedy were, once again, ascendant following the success of movies such as *Moonstruck* (Jewison, 1987) and *Broadcast News* (Brooks, 1987).

Published in 1994, Paul's study of gross-out movies concluded with the observation that the oeuvre was becoming 'fully consigned to history' (1994: 430). Twelve years later, however, gross-out returned with a vengeance following the success of *American Pie* and the procession of vulgar teen comedies that ensued. And, in some respects at least, the new arrivals seemed set on 'Going Too Far', determinedly pushing at cultural boundaries in a way that seemed to echo the earlier gross-out traditions.

A 'Near-Encyclopedic Array of Cum, Puke and Shit Gags': *American Pie* and the carnivalesque

The success of *American Pie* marked a conspicuous return for gross-out aesthetics. As film critic Stephen Holden noted (somewhat dolefully) in his review for the *New York Times*, the movie's relish for vulgarity would prompt a flurry of teenage debate – 'Which scene is the grossest? The beer scene? The pie scene? The toilet scene?' (Holden, 1999). And, certainly, *American Pie* has many of the outrageous trademarks of gross-out comedy. Missing, however, are the overtly anti-authoritarian elements that made *Animal House* such a triumph for writers such as William Paul and Tony Hendra. In *American Pie*, there are no despotic college deans to kick against, no goody-goody fraternities to wreak havoc upon. Superficially, at least, there is no aura of rebellion, no spirit of defiance. At the same time, however, it may be possible to identify *some* elements of transgression in *American Pie*'s sheer enthusiasm for the tasteless. Indeed, more generally, the vulgar teen comedy's passion for pushing at the boundaries of taste might be seen as a form of challenge to established orthodoxies and prevailing social hierarchies. In making sense of these issues, many writers have turned to the ideas of Mikhail Bakhtin.

Writing during the 1920s and 1930s, Bakhtin, a Russian semiotician and literary scholar, is most widely known for his influential study of European popular culture during the Middle Ages. This was a world, Bahktin suggests, that was strictly hierarchical and based on firm ideas of order and rank. At specific moments of carnival and festival, however, the usual hierarchies and restrictions were suspended, allowing the forbidden and the fantastic to become momentarily possible. These 'carnivalesque' spaces, Bakhtin argues, saw established systems of morality give way to an eruption of the vulgar and the irreverent, with a ritual inversion and degradation of dominant norms. As Bakhtin explains, the carnival is characterised by 'the lowering of all that is high, spiritual, ideal, abstract; it is a transfer to the material level; to the sphere of earth and the body in their indissoluble unity' (1984: 19–20).

The carnival, then, was a time of 'grotesque realism', a moment of excess, inversion, disrespect and parody that was manifest in activities such as exuberant feasting, drunkenness, mockery of authority, cross-dressing and sexual licence. And, for Bakhtin, this inversion of prevailing morality was underscored by a celebration of the corpulent excesses of the 'lower body strata'. Rejecting the controlled, disciplined body associated with the forces of propriety and authority, the 'carnivalesque' instead celebrates 'the lower stratum of the body, the life of the belly and the reproductive organs; it therefore relates to acts of defecation and copulation and pregnancy and birth' (21). Popular laughter, moreover, was always a fixture of the carnival's enthusiasm for bodily transgressions. As Bakhtin puts it:

> The people's laughter which characterized all forms of grotesque realism from immemorial times was linked with bodily lower stratums. Laughter degrades and materializes.

> (19–20)

Obviously, the carnival's original moments of inversion and transgression are long gone, but Bakhtin's ideas have been embraced by many social theorists in their analyses of more recent cultural phenomena.[2] Eric Schaefer, for example, sees the exploitation films of the 1920s and 1930s as distinctly 'carnivalesque' in the way they offered of a sensationalized exhibition of the taboo (see Chapter 3). Like Bakhtin's episodes of carnival, Schaefer argues, early exploitation movies 'privilege the "lower body stratum"' and 'overturn a classical aesthetics based on formal harmony and good taste' (Schaefer, 1999: 122). As a consequence, he suggests, these films' spectacle of the forbidden and the taboo presented a 'challenge to the system of orderly presentation of material to well-mannered spectators that was encouraged by Hollywood' (134). And, while movies such as *American Pie* are a world away from the decidedly *outré* exploitation films documented by Schaefer, vulgar teen comedies might also be considered 'carnivalesque' in the way their penchant for gross-out extremes poses a challenge to notions of the orderly and the well-mannered.

Indeed, William Paul sees clear echoes of Bakhtin's ideas in gross-out cinema. 'Gross-out films', he argues, 'have a good deal in common with Bakhtin's idea of "grotesque realism"'. Like Bakhtin's eruptions of bodily excess, Paul contends, gross-out's immersion in 'emphatic physicality' amounts to 'a deliberate reversal, an intentional lowering of the high and the spiritual' (Paul, 1994: 46). Geoff King, too, sees 'striking similarities' between Bakhtin's notion of the carnivalesque and gross-out comedy (King, 2002: 65). The historical and cultural gulf separating the traditional carnival and the aesthetics of modern-day gross-out mean the two should not be overly conflated, yet King sees distinctly carnivalesque dimensions in the way gross-out comedies 'seek to evoke a response based on transgression of what is usually allowed in "normal" or "polite" society' (67). In these terms, gross-out comedy is redolent of the rituals and revelry of the carnival in the way it violates conventional cultural norms. Like Bakhtin's unruly festivals, gross-out humour breaches the boundaries normally dividing the 'private' and the 'public'; it wantonly transgresses everyday tastes and raucously celebrates the 'grotesque realism' of bodily fluids and excretion.

American Pie stands as an apposite example. As one reviewer notes, the film features a 'near-encyclopedic array of cum, puke and shit gags' (Leigh, 1999). The 'grotesque realism' of 'bodily lower stratums' is particularly inescapable in Jim Levenstein's disastrous onanist endeavors, outrageous spectacles that not only pepper the first *American Pie* movie, but are a recurring theme in the *Pie* franchise as a whole.

American Pie 2, for instance, sees Jim kicking back for an evening of pleasuring himself to a porn video. Experimenting with a big dollop of sexual lubricant, things initially seem promising ('Woah. What have I been missing?'). But it soon becomes apparent that Jim has mistaken a tube of super-glue for the lube, leaving his hand resolutely stuck to his crotch. And, as he vainly struggles for release, his other hand becomes securely fastened to the porn movie's box. After a series of mishaps, a change of scene then reveals Jim – accompanied by his ever-patient dad – in hospital, dejectedly sitting in a queue for medical attention, with one hand cemented to his manhood and the other glued to the box for a porn film conspicuously titled *Pussy Palace*.

More misfortune features in *American Reunion*. Now married, Jim and Michelle's sex life has become humdrum in the wake of parenthood. So, while Michelle takes a bath and their two-year-old son – Evan – falls asleep, Jim seizes the opportunity to squirt copious amounts of lubricant into a sports sock and starts 'whacking off' to porn on his laptop computer. At first Jim is lost in sexual reverie, but is abruptly startled when he notices a quizzical Evan standing before him. As Jim frantically tries to close the porn, he slams the laptop shut on his penis and, crying out in agony, throws the lube-filled sock onto his bewildered toddler's head.

Alongside this zeal for 'emphatic physicality', the 'Bakhtinian' preoccupation with excreted bodily fluids that is so evident in *American Pie* also continues in subsequent releases. *American Pie 2*, for example, finds Stifler amorously pursuing the pretty Christy (Joanna Garcia) at a party. Drunk on Stifler's exotic punch, Christy seems to be falling easy prey to the Stifmeister's wiles. Decamping to the veranda, the flirty Christy prepares to pour champagne into Stifler's open mouth as he reclines, eyes closed, on a divan. Then, however, Christy is knocked out cold by a falling flower pot, clumsily knocked over by the MILF Guys on the balcony above. And, as Stifler waits expectantly below, one of the MILF Guys (John Cho) begins to relieve himself distractedly. As a steady arc of urine splashes down on Stifler's face, he sighs in ecstasy – 'Ohhh! That's it. Bathe the Stifmeister!'. Leaning back, eyes still shut, he luxuriates under the shower of piss, washing it through his hair and eagerly drinking it in – 'How did you get it so nice and warm?'. Gradually, however, he senses something is amiss – 'Oh, I can taste the bubbles...Hmm. Actually, I can't'. Then, as a mystified Stifler opens his eyes, he turns to see the unconscious Christy lying behind him and realisation swiftly dawns – 'Oh fuck!'

Indeed, Stifler himself can be seen as a kind of carnivalesque anti-hero, or 'trickster'. As Geoff King observes, the trickster is a common figure in the myths and stories of many cultures (especially those of indigenous Americans). Rowdy and disruptive, the trickster is generally 'an unruly male figure who breaks the rules, is governed by uncontrollable urges for food and sex and who often lacks a sense of unity and control over his own body parts' (King, 2002: 64). For King, the trickster can be seen as a forerunner of modern comedic figures who throw the normal order into disarray. The character of Bluto (John Belushi) in *National Lampoon's Animal House* is, King suggests, a good example, representing 'an unkempt trickster of seemingly unquenchable appetite for food, drink, sex and general mayhem' (69). In *American Pie*, Stifler is cast from a similar mold. Played superbly by Seann William Scott, Stifler is an uncontainable, inexhaustible presence. Describing himself as the 'Grand Facilitator', Stifler is a mischievous Lord of Misrule. He can conceive and stage-manage the most appalling scenarios, and his drunken parties and salacious escapades drive forward much of the film's action. An archetypal trickster, the Stifmeister is governed by his twin passions – partying and womanising. He is, moreover, profoundly obnoxious and crass, and cuts a splendidly grotesque figure with his braying laugh, wild eyes and wide, toothy grin (see Figure 4.2).

Even Stifler's speech – much of it improvised by Scott – has a carnivalesque inflection. For Bakhtin, the language of the carnival is 'Billingsgate' – the vulgar tongue of the marketplace, where the niceties of polite society and official culture are ousted by oaths, curses, strings of abuse and a slew of comical, unexpected images (Bakhtin, 1984: 16–17). And Stifler demonstrates masterful Billingsgate skills

Figure 4.2 Behold, the Stifmeister!

in his spurts of imaginative profanity, expressed in either acerbic but irrepressibly cheerful put-downs ('Happy fuck day, assmouth!') or expansive displays of self-confident hubris ('Wipe my ass and lick my balls! It's Stifler time, baby! Woo-hoo-hoo!'). Indeed, according to screenwriter Adam Herz, there are two key facets to 'Stifler Speak', and both evoke the tenor of Bahktinian Billingsgate:

> First of all, whatever's on your mind, you say it. There is no internal censor. There is no filter.

And, alongside this stream of unruly consciousness, an intrusion by wildly creative invective explodes the ordered civility of everyday manners. As Herz explains:

> You take two unrelated terms. One of them is really nasty, and one of them is completely innocuous. So 'cock' and 'lunch' becomes 'cock-lunch'. And you say it as if it's the best thing you ever thought of.[3]

Nevertheless, for all his wanton, unabashed offensiveness, Stifler (like many carnivalesque tricksters) also exudes a winsome charm. His incurable optimism and unbounded energy – coupled with the sheer, mind-boggling scope of his vulgarity – give the Stifmeister a beguiling, charismatic quality. Indeed, this allure probably explains his increasing centrality within the *American Pie* saga. In the first film Stifler was a relatively secondary figure and Seann William Scott was billed eighth in the movie credits. But, by the third instalment (*American Wedding*), Stifler's role in the plot had mushroomed and Scott had leaped to second billing. His character, meanwhile, smirked out prominently from the movie's promotional poster.

'The Lowering of All That Is High'

The carnivalesque inversion of prevailing tastes, therefore, is central to the gross-out humour characteristic of vulgar teen comedies like *American Pie*. Whether this kind of transgression amounts a subversion of established power structures, however, is moot. For Bakhtin, and many of those influenced by his ideas, the carnivalesque has definite radical and liberating potential in the way it disrupts dominant norms. Other critics, however, have argued that the carnivalesque works to *maintain* rather than subvert prevalent social relations. From this perspective the carnival acts as a kind of 'safety valve' that allows a controlled and temporary release of social tension. The carnivalesque, in these terms, represents a *licensed* form of eruption that ultimately acts as a strategy of containment. Any challenge to the status quo is marginal or temporary and is ultimately recuperated by the social order. As the cultural theorist Umberto Eco puts it:

> Carnival can exist only as an authorised transgression ... comedy and the carnival are not instances of real transgressions: on the contrary, they represent paramount examples of law reinforcement. They remind us of the existence of the rule. (Eco, 1984: 6)

Such a view, however, may be unduly pessimistic. For example, in the case of the progenitors of gross-out comedy – the 'sick' comedians of the 1950s and the 'Boomer humor' of *The National Lampoon* – it is certainly possible to identify meaningful dimensions of radical challenge. Their elements of politically-conscious parody, and their close relation to wider social liberation movements of the period, give them an unmistakably seditious edge.

But it seems harder to identify traces of subversion in the vulgar teen comedies of the late 1990s and 2000s. *American Pie*'s young heroes, for instance, are not railing against social injustice or challenging corrupt authority figures. Instead, they are on a more hedonistic quest for self-fulfillment via the heady thrills of sexual adventure and keg parties. Rather than radical and rebellious, then, their world seems self-serving and individualistic.

Nevertheless, *American Pie* is not simply a throwback to the conservative self-interest of the more banal vulgar teen comedies from the late 1980s. As King notes, cinematic moments of gross-out 'often manifest the carnivalesque dynamic of bringing down that which has pretensions to "higher" things, or that which is variously scheming, manipulative or dishonest' (King, 2002: 66). And this is certainly the case in *American Pie*, where the pompous and the vainglorious are invariably the butt of the joke. In the first *American Pie* movie, for example, the pretentious Finch is brought rudely down to earth after spreading deceitful rumours of his sexual prowess. Consequently, after his mochaccino is spiked with laxative by a vengeful Stifler, Finch's explosive diarrhoea propels him to the girls' toilet and his reputation for sophistication is (temporarily) left in tatters. It is Stifler, however, who is most usually cast as the deserving victim. With his nefarious schemes for seduction and over-the-top claims to 'alpha male' virility, the Stifmeister marks himself out as an inevitable target for the carnivalesque 'lowering of all that is high'. Hence, Stifler is the victim of both the 'beer scene' in *American Pie* and the 'champagne scene' in *American Pie 2*.

And equal degradation follows in the subsequent movies. In *American Wedding*, for instance, Stifler meets an ignominious fate when he feigns virtue and integrity in a disreputable attempt to score with the bride's sister. The pretence sees Stifler entrusted with the wedding ring, but it is lost when he unintentionally feeds it to the family's little dog. After spending the whole day waiting, Stifler finally retrieves the ring when the dog defecates. But, before he can sneak the ring back to his hotel room, he is intercepted by the bride's parents. Mistaking the dog stool in Stifler's hand for a chocolate truffle, Michelle's mother – who adores chocolate – attempts to take it, giving Stifler no other choice but to shove the 'candy' into his own mouth to save face. And, as Stifler slowly chews, the bride's parents ask how the chocolate tastes ('Is it creamy?'). In response, Stifler forces a contorted, open-mouthed grin that reveals a big smear of doggie poo across his pearly white teeth.

The humour in *American Pie*, therefore, exudes a carnivalesque commitment to 'lowering all that is high'. Moreover, while *American Pie* hardly burns with radical fury, there is definitely a sense of impish mischief in the way it pushes at the boundaries of taste and savours tweaking the tail of genteel sensibilities. So, while *American Pie* is no font of militant subversion, neither is it a wellspring of reactionary values. Instead, the movie is an ambiguous, contradictory blend of both the transgressive and the conservative, exemplifying William Paul's characterisation of gross-out as 'an art form of fissures and ambivalence' (Paul, 1994: 428). It is, though, a realm of 'fissures and ambivalence' in which some interests seem to have more authority than others given that – as Geoff King observes – films like *American Pie* 'appear to be designed to appeal principally to relatively young male audiences' (King, 2002: 73).

Wise women, amazons and sexual sorceresses: the women of *American Pie*

That vulgar teen comedies privilege male experience should be of little surprise. As film theorist Lesley Speed observes, young women have rarely been central to American youth movies which have, in general, worked to 'glorify male coming of age' (Speed, 2010: 830). In the vulgar teen comedy this focus has been especially pronounced, David Greven arguing that the genre characteristically 'foregrounds male sexual-performance anxieties and resolves them through a final realization of "manly" sexual prowess' (Greven, 2002: 17). For some critics, however, this masculine focus can have distinctly misogynistic overtones.

Speed is especially critical of the 1980s cycle of vulgar teen comedies. Concurring with William Paul, Speed sees these movies as representing an 'incorporated' shadow of their more radical predecessors. Lacking the liberatory drive of films such as *Animal House*, she argues, 1980s vulgar teen comedies saw 'the eclipse of countercultural aspirations by a more conservative political and economic climate and an isolation of hedonism from satire' (2010: 825). For many critics, this trend is exemplified by the chauvinism of *Porky's*, one of the films that kick-started the 1980s cycle (see Chapter 3). Tony Hendra, for example, argues that the gender stereotyping and sexual objectification of women in *Porky's* mark it out as 'irredeemably repulsive' (Hendra, 1987: 418). Randy Thiessen elaborates, arguing that *Porky's* most (in)famous scene – in which the male protagonists use a peephole to spy on girls using a high school's shower room – not only represents 'an archetypal male fantasy' (1998: 68) but also has close affinities with Laura Mulvey's (1975) notion of the 'male gaze', in which masculine power is constructed and reinforced through voyeuristic depictions of women.

Porky's was a clear influence on *American Pie*. Adam Herz, *Pie*'s screenwriter, cut his scholarly teeth writing a college paper on *Porky's* (see Chapter 2). And Kevin Maher, reviewing *American Pie* for the British Film Institute, suggests the movie clearly uses *Porky's* as a 'structural template':

> From the opening erection gag through to the alternative penetration setpiece, this bawdy account of over-excitable high-school teens who 'just gotta get laid' is surprisingly faithful to the crude episodic pay-offs of its predecessor.
>
> (Maher, n.d.)

In updating the formula of the vulgar teen comedy for the late 1990s, however, *American Pie*'s creators made a conscious effort to avoid the chauvinism evident in many of its 1980s forebears. According to Herz, a key difference between *American Pie* and its predecessors was the increased depth given to the female characters. 'I didn't want the girls to be your typical sex objects, the clichéd teen comedy stereotypes', Herz has recalled, 'So, I made sure that in whatever I wrote, I gave them as much credit, if not more, than the guys' (quoted in Siegel, 2012). *Pie* producer Chris Moore has concurred, explaining:

> The thing that I loved about Adam's script is that the girls ultimately decide who has sex in the movie. We consciously tried to

make the characters more realistic, which, by definition, means the women have to be more authentic.

(quoted in ibid.)

And *American Pie*'s directors, Chris and Paul Weitz, explicitly distanced themselves from the likes of *Porky's*. Preparing for *Pie*, the brothers had watched the earlier teen comedy but neither, Chris Weitz has recalled, could stomach it through to the end:

> It was just full of terrifying instances of misogyny.... The girls are basically ambulatory mammaries, and there's a really noticeable strain of hostility and meanness of spirit toward women running through the entire thing. And not only could you not get away with that now, I don't see why anyone would want to. We certainly didn't.
>
> (quoted in Leigh, 1999)

His brother concurred, arguing that, 'Traditionally...this kind of film was basically just guy-ogles-girl. Whereas it was important for us to express the idea that both genders are interested in sex, and girls don't have to be the passive object' (quoted in ibid.).

These concerns reflected broader trends. The late 1990s and early 2000s saw an increased prominence of girls across American popular culture, with a growing centrality of confident, independent and relatively complex female characters in movies such as *Clueless* (Heckerling, 1995), *Bring It On* (Reed, 2000) and *Mean Girls* (Waters, 2004), along with TV series such as *My So-Called Life* (ABC, 1994–1995) and *Buffy the Vampire Slayer* (WB, 1997–2001; UPN, 2002–2003).[4] These developments were partly a consequence of commercial industries' attempts to tap into new consumer markets, but, as Mary Celeste Kearney observes, they were also indebted to an influx of women and feminist ideas into the world of media production. In filmmaking, Kearney argues, this spawned a spate of movies that 'broadened the spectrum of female adolescence beyond the white, middle-class, suburban stereotype of teenage girlhood consistently reproduced by the Hollywood studios' (2002: 131).

American Pie, of course, remains a film centred on the experience of its male protagonists. But broader cultural shifts clearly impacted on its production, and, responding to the significant changes in attitudes about gender, *Pie*'s creators strove to move beyond the misogynist tone of 1980s teen comedies and incorporate stronger and more complex female characters in the movie. Indeed, it was an aspiration that meets with a degree of success. As film theorist Sarah Hentges observes, *American Pie* 'is worlds past its predecessors where girls were only allowed to be the pie, and not allowed to eat a piece for themselves' (2006: 218). Certainly, elements of traditional gender stereotypes survive, but these are undercut by the female characters' dimensions of control and sexual confidence. As Hentges explains:

> Women and girls are still portrayed in these stereotypical roles as sexual objects, but girls are also negotiating this status while simultaneously providing new sexual fronts where girls not only have power, but are also empowered, often in the process.
>
> (ibid.)

David Greven agrees. 'For such deeply male-oriented entertainments', Greven argues, 'the *American Pie* films feature remarkably distinct and memorable female characters'. While Vicky Lathum (Kevin's girlfriend) is relatively one-dimensional, the other female characters 'are sexual dynamos with breezy airs of confidence, an avid appetite for sex, and no compunctions about discussing or satisfying their sexual needs' (Greven, 2002: 17). For example, Jessica (Vicky's best friend) appears as 'a cross between wise-woman village crone and matchmaking yenta' and she 'confirms the movie's gendered schema – it is the women who control and create the realm of sex' (ibid.). Hentges goes further, arguing that Jessica is *American Pie*'s 'most empowered and autonomous female (or male) character':

> She is experienced, but she has not been obliterated by her experience; she has been made stronger. She has fallen prey to the talk and the act, but she is now free to keep her options open.... Jessica's autonomy allows her to be advisor and confidante to all of the clueless boys and girls.
>
> (Hentges, 2006: 220)

Other female characters are equally positive. Heather, Hentges argues, is 'intelligent, autonomous and self-ware' (ibid.), while erstwhile 'band geek' Michelle subverts gender stereotypes as she 'takes her sexuality into her own hands' (218). Indeed, Greven notes how the humour of the post-prom party scene in which Jim and Michelle finally get together relies on the way the paucity of Jim's sexual performance is juxtaposed to Michelle's blithe, unselfconscious move from one of her incessant, insipid 'band camp' stories to a casual revelation about her sexual adventures – 'One time, at band camp, I stuck a flute in my pussy!' (Greven, 2002: 17). And, as the action shifts to the bedroom, Michelle's wild side becomes even more evident as (in dialogue largely improvised by actor Alyson Hannigan herself) she takes domineering command of their erotic encounter – 'What's my name?! Say my name, bitch!'. As Greven concludes, therefore, Michelle is 'neither clueless nor frigid', but is 'a sexual sorceress who controls all aspects of the sexual performance' (ibid.).

Shannon Elizabeth's tall, sexy Nadia also seems self-assured and in control. Indeed, as Greven observes, in her (aborted) tryst with Jim, Nadia is 'Amazonian' in the way she towers over him, her stature attesting to the sexual confidence of the film's female characters more generally (ibid.). However, the scene in which Nadia is filmed by a hidden webcam in Jim's bedroom while she undresses and masturbates can seem disconcerting. In many respects the episode has the appearance of a textbook example of Laura Mulvey's 'male gaze', in which female film characters are coded with qualities of 'to-be-looked-at-ness', constructed as the passive objects of a privileged male spectator. The inclusion of a group of high school girls in Nadia's assorted Internet audiences is clearly intended to mitigate against this gendered positioning, but, given the heavy preponderance of surreptitious male onlookers, the connotations of a voyeuristic male gaze remain pronounced. That said, some critics have suggested alternative ways of reading Nadia's 'webcam' scene.

Placed in context, the sexual politics of the scene seem ambiguous. Initially, it is certainly the male gaze that is foremost. But, as the episode unfolds, Nadia turns the tables on Jim. 'Now you have seen me', she pouts, 'I want to see you', and she commands him to strip and dance for her. Jim's hyperactive dance routine, however, is ludicrous; his body exhibits conspicuous puppy fat and he cuts a pathetic figure clad in his unflattering boxer shorts. Jim's performance before a laughing Nadia, then, seems to challenge conventional notions of masculine power. Indeed, as media theorist Sharyn Pearce (2003) observes, the scene can be seen as reversing the usual sexual division of the gaze, with the usual inscribing of heterosexual masculinity replaced by a privileging of female spectatorship. The humour of the episode, moreover, relies on the clear contrast between Nadia's bold sexual confidence and Jim's feeble premature ejaculations. From this perspective, therefore, rather than being a straightforward illustration of Mulvey's 'male gaze', the episode is actually conflicted and contradictory. Relatively open-ended, it can be interpreted in a variety of ways, including some that challenge traditional gender positions. As Pearce explains:

> However one chooses to 'read' the scene, it is evident that it if, as Mulvey suggests, the film text constructs its spectators through

Figure 4.3 Jim dances for Nadia – 'Oh yeah, I'm naughty. I'm naughty, baby'.

processes that can be mapped onto the unconscious structures through which our gendered identities are produced, then in this instance, as in others, *American Pie* constructs a space for opposition and change and for alternative audience positioning. In setting up the audience to share the spectators' look, the orthodox gendered alignment of looking, masculinity and power is clearly being undermined. (see Figure 4.3)

(Pearce, 2003: 73)

This kind of challenge to masculine authority can, indeed, be seen as a recurring theme in *American Pie*. As writer Roz Kaveney observes, there is invariably an element of 'revenge' to the repeated degradation of the film's male characters, and 'one of the reasons we enjoy as comic the humiliations heaped on Jim and the others is that they are the deserved consequences of thoughtless humiliation of the women they are involved with' (Kaveney, 2006: 146).

American Pie, however, can hardly brag impeccably 'feminist' credentials. Undoubtedly, as Hentges notes, the movie's representation of women moves beyond the stock duality of previous teen films in which 'a character with slutty characteristics, like behavior or dress, is punished and the virginal, in behavior or appearance, is rewarded' (Hentges, 2006: 216). Yet, as David Greven argues, the 'sorceress-like power' wielded by *American Pie*'s women actually works to fetishise the characters and marginalises them from the film's narrative. In common with other vulgar teen comedies of the period, Greven suggests, *American Pie*'s female characters are configured as 'remote goddesses' who exert a detached influence over proceedings but actively participate relatively little:

> Assigning all the sexual power to the women and girls, then, becomes a means of containing and entrapping female experience – their confidence in these films serves as consolation prizes, concessions to the rising social prominence of women that yet manage to keep femaleness out of the narrative trajectory of individual life.
>
> (Greven, 2002: 18)

In the *American Pie* sequels, moreover, the female characters seem to become even more peripheral. In *American Pie 2*, for example, Michelle gradually loses her eccentric traits and singular conversational rhythms as she becomes romantically smitten with Jim – a process which, as Greven observes, is common in Hollywood movies, which 'force women to give up their distinctiveness in order to realize romantic love' (ibid.). Nadia's 'Amazonian' strength is also much denuded. In the sequel she returns as a more neurotic and insecure version of her former self and, rebuffed by Jim (who now realizes he loves Michelle), she is reduced to seeking solace by deflowering the arch-geek, Chuck 'The Shermanator' Sherman. Vicky, meanwhile, returns more sexually confident than previously, but barely figures in the movie at all. And Heather, relegated to a year abroad in Europe, also scarcely registers as a presence. Indeed, in the third instalment (*American Wedding*) Vicky and Heather, along with Nadia, disappear altogether. As a consequence, Hentges concludes (somewhat disappointedly), the three initial *American Pie* films 'are not, ultimately, an example of empowered sexuality for girls and women, unless we consider their near escape from the trilogy as empowering' (Hentges, 2006: 223).

The female characters reappear, however, in *American Pie*'s fourth theatrical instalment, *American Reunion*. And Michelle, at least, recaptures some of her former spark. For instance, as she relaxes by the lakeside with her best friend from high school, Selena (Dania Raminez), we are reminded of Michelle's wild side as she nonchalantly reminisces:

MICHELLE: Hey, remember that one time, at band camp, when we licked whipped cream off each other's…
SELENA: [Hurriedly interrupting] Yes, yes. I remember….

And, at Stifler's reunion party, as Jim and Michelle retire to the bedroom for some sexual role-play to reignite their love-life, their choice of costume is telling. Jim is clad as a 'gimp', wearing black, PVC hotpants and a leather dog-collar. Michelle, meanwhile, appears in full dominatrix regalia, with knee-high boots, cleavage bulging from a tight leather dress and her red hair pulled back in a severe pony-tail. Moreover, when the party descends into a chaotic fist-fight between the guests and teenage gate-crashers, it is Michelle who wades in to defend her beleaguered spouse. As a gimp-attired Jim wrestles on the ground with a burly youth, Michelle (in her intimidating dominatrix outfit) steams into the fray, beating the teen with a riding crop and berating him fiercely – 'Get off my husband, you little piece of shit!'.

Beneath Michelle's meek, 'band geek' exterior, then, there always bubbles a feisty 'sexual sorceress'. In this capacity, Michelle is redolent of the carnivalesque figure of 'the unruly woman' or 'the woman on top'. Whereas Bakhtin's own study of the carnival focused primarily on issues of social class, a number of feminist theorists have extended his carnivalesque principles to the realm of gender, arguing that, across history, the model of 'the unruly woman' has represented a disruptive challenge to prevailing gender relations. For the historian Natalie Zemon Davis (1965), notions of 'women on top' were especially evident in the carnivals of pre-modern Europe where they represented a particularly disruptive presence given the degree to which those societies' rigidly hierarchical thinking was underpinned by assumptions of women's subservience to men. In this context, Davis argues, 'the unruly woman' was an ambiguous figure. On one hand, she could be seen as 'shameful and outrageous', a nagging harridan to be muzzled and ducked in the local pond. But, on the other hand, she could also be championed as 'vigorous and in command' (Davis, 1965: 140). Emphasising the importance of this facet of rebellion, Davis explains:

> The image of the disorderly woman did not always function to keep women in their place. On the contrary, it was a multivalent image that could operate, first, to widen behavioral options for women within and even outside marriage, and second, to sanction riot and political disobedience for both men and women in a society that allowed the lower orders few formal means of protest. Play with an unruly woman is partly a chance for temporary release from the traditional and stable hierarchy; but it is also part of the conflict over efforts to change the basic distribution of power within society.
> (Davis, 1965: 131)

Davis tracks 'the woman on top' across a range of cultural texts of the early modern period, finding examples in paintings and theatrical productions as well as in books, proverbs and poems. But Kathleen Rowe argues the trope also remains evident in many contemporary contexts, and 'reverberates whenever women disrupt the norms of femininity and the social hierarchy of male over female through excess and outrageousness' (Rowe, 1995: 30). Rowe's preeminent modern-day examples are the comedian Roseanne Barr and Miss Piggy, the porcine virago from The Muppets. But the image is also, at least partially, manifest in *American Pie*'s Michelle Flaherty. Funny, confident and sexually adventurous, Michelle seems to embody Rowe's account of unruly women as those who 'allow their "lower" unruly impulses to control their "higher" ones; giving rein to the "wild" lower part of [themsleves] and seeking power over others' (35). Indeed, in the scene where Jim ultimately loses his virginity, it is very much Michelle who is – both literally and figuratively – 'the woman on top' (see Figure 4.4).

This representation of feisty femininity, however, does not mean that *American Pie* presents a resolute challenge to gendered power relations. As Rowe points out, '[c]arnival and the unruly woman are not essentially radical but are ambivalent, open to conflicting appropriations' (44). In these terms, then, *American Pie* certainly moves away from the casual chauvinism that characterised many of the 1980s vulgar teen comedies – but, rather than comprising a coherent and consistent set of ideological positions, it is shot-through with contradictions and spaces for audience interpretation and reinterpretation.

Figure 4.4 Michelle (Alyson Hannigan) gets her way – 'What's my name?! Say my name, bitch!'

As such, *American Pie* neatly attests to William Paul's view of gross-out movies as 'an art form of fissures and ambivalence'.

American Pie's theatrically-released sequels also exhibit this sense of 'fissures and ambivalence'. But the quality is much less evident in the *American Pie Presents…*direct-to-DVD films. Released between *American Wedding* and *American Reunion*, the four direct-to-DVD movies feature new actors and characters, and have tenuous relation to their big screen brethren (see Chapter 3). Moreover, without the budgets or creative talent of the theatrically-released films, the straight-to-DVD movies are poor by comparison. They are shoddily written, full of lazy stereotypes and have set-piece gags whose punch-lines are telegraphed several days in advance. More than this, however, the attitude of the DVD movies often seems boorish and obnoxious rather than mischievously transgressive. Like the theatrical movies, they push at boundaries of taste but – without any sense of ambivalence or tongue-in-cheek wit – they often seem to be offensive simply for the sake of it. Much of the humour of *American Pie Presents: The Naked Mile*, for instance, is derived from the fierce rivalry between Dwight Stifler's college fraternity and their adversaries, a fraternity composed entirely of dwarves – and this can make for uncomfortable viewing.[5]

It is the sexual politics of *Pie*'s direct-to-DVD releases, however, that are especially unpleasant. Not only are the female characters few, they also lack depth and seem to exist simply as passive sexual objects; submissive foils to the boys' lustful tomfoolery. Indeed, the *American Pie Presents…*DVD movies seem like a sad regression to the chauvinistic teen comedies of the 1980s. Indicative is 'Band Camp Girls: The Music Video', a bonus feature included with *American Pie Presents: Band Camp*, which sees the film's female characters perform a raunchy dance routine to Sir Mix-a-Lot's hip-hop anthem, 'I Like Big Butts' – all seemingly delivered without a trace of irony.

The conservative and chauvinistic overtones of *Pie*'s direct-to-DVD releases, however, should not overshadow the more complex, carnivalesque qualities of the theatrically-released entries in the *American Pie* franchise. As this chapter has demonstrated, the gross-out humour central to vulgar teen comedies such as *American Pie* has a long history in US popular culture and, while this humour is distinguished by a distinct sense of ambivalence, it also often offers important spaces for cultural transgression and disruption. But, as well as being characterised by their taste for the outrageous excesses of gross-out humour, vulgar teen comedies such as *American Pie* are also denoted by their construction of young people and youth culture. This is an area to which attention turns in the next chapter.

Notes

1 For Hendra (1987: 421–2), the nadir of this trend came with the *Police Academy* film series. Beginning in 1984 with *Police Academy* (Wilson), the movie franchise relied on a mixture of low-brow humour, sexual innuendo and physical comedy. Running to a total of seven theatrical releases, the last in the series was 1994's *Police Academy: Mission to Moscow* (Metter).

2 Examples of studies that use Bakhtin's theories to analyse modern-day cultural texts include Docker (1994), Fiske (1989), Glynn (2000) and Stam (1992).

3 See 'Stifler Speak', a bonus feature included on the 2001 DVD release of *American Pie 2*.

4 Before she appeared in *American Pie* as 'band geek' Michelle Flaherty, actor Alyson Hannigan was already established in the TV series *Buffy the Vampire Slayer*, playing nerdy teen witch, Willow Rosenberg.

5 To be fair, however, the scene featuring a brutal football game between the rival fraternities is well choreographed and has some amusing moments. And, while few, there are still a handful of laughs in the other direct-to-DVD *Pie* movies. *American Pie Presents: Beta House*, for example, includes a fairly funny gross-out pastiche of the 'Russian roulette' scene from *The Deer Hunter* (Cimino, 1978).

5 'High school was awesome'

Constructions of youth in *American Pie*

Performing youth in *American Pie*

'We were enormous fans of that first *American Pie*', recall Jon Hurwitz and Hayden Schlossberg, the writer-director team behind the *Pie* series' fourth instalment, *American Reunion*. 'We were in college when it came out', Hurwitz remembers, 'and we watched it over and over and over again. We knew the characters and the franchise really, really well'. The gross-out gags were part of the appeal but, as Hurwitz explains, also important was the movie's treatment of the experiences and relationships of youth:

> What we loved about the original *American Pie* was the fact that, yes, Jim had sex with a pie, but it also dealt with first love and father-son relationships, and things like that.... There's a core friendship with the guys, which has a lot of heart, and there's the father-son relationship and all the love stories that it brings, too.
>
> (quoted in Radish, 2012)

The way *American Pie* configures its characters' relationships and identities represents a distinctive *performance* of youth. The concept of performance was originally developed in Judith Butler's post-structuralist theories of gender. For Butler, gender categories are multiform and historically variable rather than monolithic and timelessly fixed. Gender, Butler argues, should not be conceived as a stable identity or an 'agency from which various acts follow', but instead should be recognized as 'an identity tenuously constituted in time, instituted in an exterior space through a stylized repetition of acts' (Butler, 1990: 140). According to Butler, then, gender should be understood as a historically dynamic 'performance' – a system of cultural conventions that is fabricated and sustained through 'a process of iterability, a regularized and constrained repetition of norms' (Butler, 1993: 95).

From this perspective, *American Pie*'s characters do not articulate any inherent, intrinsic gender qualities. Instead, they deliver a distinctive performance of gender, articulating specific notions of masculinity and femininity forged in a particular historical and cultural context. Indeed, the models of masculinity embodied in Jim Levenstein and his buddies are an apposite example of the way masculinity, as Steven Cohan and Ina Rae Hark put it, 'is an effect of culture and construction, a performance, a masquerade rather than a universal and unchanging essence' (1993: 7). Moreover, as Frances Smith argues, 'youth', itself, can be considered a 'performative' category. While Butler does not, herself, address the cultural construction of youth, Smith suggests the idea of gender as a 'stylized repetition of acts' chimes with 'the ephemerality and liminality of teenage gender identity, and adolescence more generally' (Smith, 2017: 5). In these terms, then, *American Pie* delivers a distinctly gendered, culturally-constructed performance of youth.

This chapter explores the performance of youth in *American Pie*. It begins by considering the way the film marked a shift in Hollywood 'coming-of-age' movies through its combination of a more explicit treatment of teen sexuality and a greater emphasis on empathy and emotional transition. The chapter then examines the ways that the 'America' in *American Pie* is coded in terms of a particular kind of ethnicity and class. The film, it is argued, maintains the traditions of Hollywood teen cinema through its depiction of youth culture as essentially white and middle-class. At the same time, however, recognition is given to the place of the *Pie* movies in a 'new wave' of Jewish filmmaking, and the way representations of the Levenstein family point to a wider reconfiguration of Jewishness in contemporary cinema. Attention then turns to *American Pie*'s configuration of young masculinity. The film's distinctive treatment of male friendship is highlighted, together with the way the movies' representations of masculinity relate to broader historical shifts in masculine identities. The chapter concludes by considering the 'nostalgic mood' of *American Pie*, and the way a distinct sense of melancholia surrounds the *Pie* movies' portrayal of the transience youth. While there are hints of this in the first movie, the tone becomes more explicit in *American Reunion*, encapsulated by Steve Stifler (now a disgruntled thirty-something) who bemoans the passing of youth in his own, inimitable style:

High school was awesome. But then we graduated and everybody started getting married and all that other stupid crap.

Virgin territory: sexuality and coming-of-age in *American Pie*

American Pie's focus on Jim and his buddies' journey to sexual maturity has conspicuously Oedipal overtones. Jim's congress with his mother's apple pie, the sexual allure of Stifler's Mom and the kids' abiding ardour for MILFs, all point towards distinctly psychoanalytic themes. But the friends' desperate quest for sexual experience also exemplifies tropes central to teen cinema. Like many youth films, *American Pie* configures adolescence as a time of physical and (especially) emotional coming-of-age, a period of transition marked by distinctive rites-of-passage that signpost young people's progression to maturity and adulthood. And, given the significance of puberty and sexual development to social and cultural constructions of adolescence, these are issues that are almost inevitably conspicuous in the narratives of teen movies. As Catherine Driscoll argues, 'Because puberty, gender and sex are crucial to adolescence there is no such thing as a teen film that does not include sex, even if there is no sex on screen' (2011: 71). Indeed, for Frances Smith the sexual coming-of-age narrative represents 'the primary determinant of what constitutes the Hollywood teen movie' (2017: 18). As a consequence, virginity – and its loss – is a theme that looms large in teen cinema, and its representation invariably encapsulates not only notions of personal identity development but also shifting social assumptions about age, gender and sexuality. As Driscoll explains:

> Virginity is an important recurring element of teen film for several reasons. It is one place in which to see the negotiation of individual choice and socially established norms. It intersects historically specific and highly gendered experiences of adolescence with political opposition between tradition and change.
>
> (2011: 71)

Hollywood's representation of teen sexuality, however, was significantly limited until well after the end of the Production Code in 1968. Before this, sexually active adolescents tended to be framed as a social danger, as in the case of many delinquency pictures of the 1950s. Alternatively, sexuality was played down in favour of the sugary romances that characterised 'clean teenpics' such as AIP's *Beach Party* series of the early 1960s (see Chapter 3). After the Production Code's demise, explicit sexual themes became commonplace in mainstream cinema, but teenage sexuality remained a sensitive topic and change registered more slowly in youth films. By the early 1980s, however, things were changing, and Timothy Shary contends 'large and small studios flooded the market with depictions of teens' rowdy and occasionally educational forays into sexual practice' (Shary, 2014: 223). The 'slasher' cycle of 1980s horror movies, for instance, became infamous for a somewhat tormented treatment of teen sexuality, with nubile youngsters apparently 'punished' for their active sexuality.[1] But, beyond the slasher movies, many other movies represented teenage sexual adventures as 'apparently playful, humorous, and ultimately safe' (222). Vulgar teen comedies such as *National Lampoon's Animal House* and *Porky's* were obviously in the vanguard, while Shary notes how, after *Fast Times at Ridgemont High* became a hit in 1982, 'the losing virginity plot became dominant in American youth cinema' (252).

Positive framings of teen sexuality, however, significantly receded during the late 1980s. As Thomas Doherty points out, upbeat representations of teenage sexual exploits disappeared as 'AIDS, the horror nascent in real-life sex, reshaped the moral landscape of the teenpic genre' (2002: 198). Shary concurs, arguing that growing social anxieties around issues such as AIDS and teenage pregnancies ensured that American teen cinema made a distinct move away from the sexualized images of youth that had dominated the screen in the early 1980s. Instead, film narratives either focused on romantic pre-sexual relationships among teens or displaced depictions of teenage sexuality into more 'innocent' eras – a strategy exemplified by such movies as *Peggy Sue Got Married* (Coppola, 1986) and *La Bamba* (Valdez, 1987) (Shary, 2014: 223–4). The trend remained prevalent throughout the 1990s and ensured that, as Shary observes, '[n]early a decade elapsed in which the losing virginity film appeared to have vanished' (258).

Nevertheless, the general resurgence of teen cinema during the late 1990s (see Chapter 3) brought a revival of the losing virginity narrative. It could, however, be framed from a variety of perspectives. Shary notes, for example, how a more negative depiction featured in movies such as *Cruel Intentions* (Kumble, 1999), where sexual conquest is represented as having potentially dire consequences (2014: 260–1). In contrast, *American Pie* offered a much more affirmative, light-hearted spin on the theme.

American Pie, however, did not simply mark a return to the prurient antics of the 1980s teen romps. Many critics, for example, highlight *Pie*'s stronger, more independent female characters (see Chapter 4). Moreover, the twists in the movie's plot provide a sense of gender balance missing from earlier teen comedies. As Shary observes, in the course of the film Jim and his buddies come to realise 'that their horny desires will take them nowhere, and the girls they pursue want more than to be chased: they want a level of affection and attention not accorded to teen girls in many previous sex comedies' (2014: 262). In contrast to the vulgar teen comedies of the 1980s, then, *American Pie*'s 'coming-of-age' narrative does not simply revolve around sexual experience and the loss of virginity. Rather, the movie's 'rites-of-passage' are represented by the acquisition of empathy, respect for others and an appreciation of personal relationships. Indeed, as Shary notes, there is a distinctly 'redemptive' dimension to the boy's fulfillment of their virginity pact:

> ...as the boys move toward the climactic first times, they each earn a modicum of self-esteem by rising above their initially base impulses and learning to treat the self-assured girls with respect, so that all of their eventual sex scenes are rendered tender and/ or humorous, and further, they are all ultimately celebratory, a phenomenon that had been minimized in American youth films for over a decade.
>
> (ibid.)

While *American Pie* was certainly influenced by the vulgar teen comedies of the 1980s, then, its sexual politics marked a move away from the raunchy chauvinism of movies like *Porky's*. In contrast to its forerunners, *American Pie*'s coming-of-age narrative does not simply hinge on sexual conquests by self-absorbed young men. Instead, it encompasses dimensions of emotional transition in which the characters learn to appreciate and value others' feelings. This is underscored towards the end of the movie, when Jim and his buddies meet up in a diner the morning after Stifler's post-prom party. Their sexual pact is now successfully concluded, but their mood is hardly victorious. There is no crowing or back-slapping. Instead, the boys are quiet and reflective. As Kenneth Kidd argues, therefore, in contrast to *Porky's* and its ilk, *American Pie* 'represents a kinder, gentler sort of teen film, one that emphasizes romance, responsibility, and male vulnerability' (Kidd, 2004: 107).

Despite its differences, *American Pie* is similar to earlier teen movies in the way the high school senior prom figures as a coming-of-age milestone. A formal dance held in the final days before graduation, the prom has iconic status in American culture. As Amy Best demonstrates in her history of the event, the prom has become entrenched as a rite-of-passage 'in which teens make sense of what it means to be young in culture today, negotiate the process of schooling, solidify their social identities, and struggle against the structural limits in which they find themselves' (Best, 2000: 2). Given its important place in American youth culture, it should be of little surprise that the prom has figured prominently across Hollywood teen movies, Shary observing how 'a strikingly high percentage of youth films have depicted the "big dance" as either a crucial event or driving force in their stories' (2014: 227). Smith agrees and highlights the particular prominence of the prom in the Hollywood school movie, arguing that 'the prom often provides the site of its denouement, demonstrating both the conclusion of the characters' high school experience and, with it, their progression into adulthood' (2017: 65). For Smith, moreover, teen cinema's depictions of the prom are 'heavily freighted with ideological baggage' (ibid.). Basing her analysis on the movies *Pretty in Pink*, *She's All That* and *Mean Girls*, Smith argues that cinematic representations of the prom (like the event itself) work to reproduce dominant notions of gender and sexuality and characteristically serve, as Smith puts it, as a locus of 'heteronormative gender interpellation' (2017: 66).

At the same time, however, Smith resists seeing the teen movie prom as an ideological steamroller. Dominant notions of gender and sexuality may figure prominently in representations of the high school prom, but, Smith argues, individual characters are invariably able to find ways to negotiate their subjectivity so that, while representations of the teen prom are 'extremely normative spaces', it is still possible 'to identify sites of resistance and complexity within those spaces' (102).

And, to a degree, *American Pie*'s depiction of the prom is also a site of 'resistance and complexity'. Superficially, *Pie*'s prom seems like a prime example of 'heteronormative gender interpellation'. The guys are all with their dates (aside for the disconsolate Finch), and the kids' dinner jackets and evening dresses exude the gendered codes and conventions of the stock high school prom. Beneath this veneer, however, there is a more ambivalent take on the prom's iconic status. As the movie's director, Paul Weitz explains, the film's creators 'wanted to come up with the lamest prom possible'. Screenwriter Adam Herz elaborates:

> As I originally wrote it – and I think it survived into the script – the band was described as 'crappy prom band'. 'Cos I hate all the movies where the prom is great and it's all about the prom. Because the prom isn't great. It's completely overrated.[2]

American Pie's prom is, to be sure, decidedly lame. Its 'Arabian Nights' theme is laughably tacky, as is its decor (gold lamé palm trees).

In addition, the band are risible and the high school kids shuffle about unenthusiastically on the dance-floor. Effectively, then, the scene is a farcical deconstruction of the prom's iconic rituals and pageantry. An ironic spoof, it sardonically sends-up the prom's mythological status in American culture. Indeed, this is a sense of irony that pervades *American Pie* as a whole.

In Hollywood cinema, Mandy Merck argues, the use of the adjective 'American' has invariably operated 'to problematize the nation it identifies'. 'As in the overarching trope of the American Dream', Merck explains, 'the national adjective can operate as both a patriotic and ironic term, sometimes suggesting the failure of an American ideal, sometimes the Americanness of failure in a highly competitive society' (Merck, 2007: 265). This 'problematisation' of traditional American values is not explicit in *American Pie*, but it is a theme that undoubtedly surfaces in the film's ambivalent portrait of youth and coming-of-age. On one hand, *American Pie* clearly revels in the rich mythologies of fun and freedom that have, since the 1950s, sedimented around representations of American teenage culture. But, at the same time, the film also ironically caricatures and critiques those mythologies. Indeed, while the film's title evokes the traditional myths of wholesome Americana – 'mom, the flag and apple pie' – director Paul Weitz has emphasized the film's elements of cultural critique, especially in its signature 'apple pie' scene:

> I like the whole idea of fucking the pie – in the States, with the apple pie family and all the baggage that goes with that concept, a kid with his dick in an apple pie is really quite an aggressively subversive image.
>
> (quoted in Leigh, 1999)

Nevertheless, while undoubtedly present, such elements of iconoclasm tend to be relatively low in the mix. Indeed, in some respects, *American Pie*'s configuration of youth culture can seem relatively conservative, especially in terms of the movie's representation of class and ethnicity.

'A Stylized Reality': class and ethnicity in *American Pie*

According to Chris Moore, the movie's co-producer, '*American Pie* is a stylized reality' (quoted in Siegel, 2012). Moore is referring to the film's larger-than-life representation of high school life, with its extraordinary characters and over-the-top scenarios. But *American Pie*'s reality is also stylized in the way it depicts youth culture as a universe of white, upper middle-class affluence. In this respect, the movie maintains traditions established in the upsurge of Hollywood youth films during the 1980s. The movies of John Hughes, especially, have been criticised for their persistent focus on white, high school suburbanites, Ann De Vaney arguing that Hughes' films are distinctly 'neoconservative' in their treatment of gender, race and class (De Vaney, 2002: 204). Shirley Steinberg and Joe Kincheloe make a similar point regarding the maverick heroes of Hughes' comedies *Weird Science* (1985) and *Ferris Bueller's Day Off* (1986). These films' free-spirited teens come from comfortable, well-heeled backgrounds, but they abruptly rebel because they have 'had enough'. 'We can only assume', Steinberg and Kincheloe observe sardonically, 'that they have had enough of living in affluent neighborhoods, having household servants and access to unlimited funds, computers, and vehicles' (Steinberg and Kincheloe, 1998: 110).

American Pie's mise-en-scène is equally bourgeois. Set around the prosperous environs of East Great Falls, its young characters live in a world of lavish mansions with manicured lawns and double (if not treble) garages. Mandy Merck makes the point eloquently:

> *American Pie*'s plotting depends on not one but two conspicuously large houses in the single-parented Stifler family, the second with its own lakeside boathouse, the scene of Oz and Heather's post-prom idyll. (Stifler's Mom, we are told, got this house in her divorce settlement.) The sequels maintain this bourgeois setting in the luxurious beach house the boys rent in *American Pie 2*, as well as in the resort hotel of *American Wedding*.
>
> (Merck, 2007: 265)

In common with many Hollywood teen movies, then, issues of social class evaporate in *American Pie*. Instead, the film's characters are uniformly well-off and middle-class, and their way of life is effectively naturalized as *the* elemental culture of American youth. Similarly, *American Pie*'s limited acknowledgment of ethnic diversity is a trait common in teen cinema.

Admittedly, issues of race and racism surfaced in the pioneering vulgar teen comedies. According to William Paul, for example, *National Lampoon's Animal House* 'has a sharp satirical sense of white culture's relation to black culture' (Paul, 1994: 128). For the most part, the few black characters in *Animal House* are on the periphery of the action. But, in a scene where the (white) fraternity boys go to an African-American nightclub to catch a rhythm 'n' blues band, the film shows how, in US culture, 'black music and musicians are invoked as a kind of prelude to uninhibitedness for whites' (129). And, while the students assume their 'hip' disposition will carry favor with the club's clientele, the atmosphere is increasingly frosty as 'the white boys who assume an automatic close-ness to blacks...are made to confront the fact that their assumptions are based on a fantasy of the actual social structure' (130).

Issues of racism also figure in *Porky's*. A subplot in the movie sees Tim (Cyril O'Reilly) – one of the film's group of libidinous buddies – configured as a vocal racist who spits bile and venom at a Jewish kid, Brian Schwartz (Scott Colomby), until his prejudice is ultimately con-fronted and cast off. Tim's bigotry, however, is depicted as the result of his being physically and verbally abused by his drunken 'white trash' father, so any sense of racism being related to more deep-rooted, struc-tural inequalities is effectively sidelined.

The 'racial' subplots in *Animal House* and *Porky's*, moreover, are relatively marginal. And themes of race and racism subsequently disappeared from view in the torrent of teen movies that followed. Indeed, writer Jonathan Bernstein suggests that 1980s teen cinema amounted to 'a triumph of ethnic cleansing', Bernstein observing how youth films of the decade were mostly populated by 'White nerds. White geeks. White jocks. White princesses. White stoners' (Bernstein, 1997: 32).

This, however, is less true of the new wave of teen movies that ap-peared from the late 1990s. Like Hollywood cinema more generally, teen movies of the 1990s showed greater sensitivity to issues of 'race' and ethnicity, and made more effort to include African-American and Asian-American characters. A number of critics, however, have argued that this was a respect in which *American Pie* fell noticeably short. Robin Wood, for example, is an enthusiastic fan of the film but still laments the way 'there isn't a single memorable black or Asian presence' (Wood, 2003: 312). Other assessments are more withering, and Merck draws an especially disparaging comparison between *American Pie* and its 1980s forerunner:

> If the Weitz brothers or their screenwriter Adam Herz remembered *Porky's* emphatic interest in race and ethnicity when they set out to modernize its sexual comedy, they certainly made no effort to address it – no conscious effort, anyway, for *American Pie* takes place in the monocultural Michigan town of East Great Falls... here the only ethnically marked teen is the Czech exchange stu-dent Nadia, who is quickly returned to her European homeland.
>
> (Merck, 2007: 268)

This criticism, however, may be a little overplayed. For, although they are certainly marginal, a handful of African-American and Asian-American characters still crop up across the *American Pie* franchise. Most obviously, Korean-American actor John Cho features as 'MILF Guy #2', a role that gradually expanded in *Pie*'s successive theatrical releases and which springboarded Cho into a successful Hollywood career.

Where ethnic diversity registers more strongly is in *American Pie*'s Jewish dimensions. Indeed, Merck identifies notable Jewish anteced-ents to the gross-out aesthetic as a whole. Most obviously, Merck ar-gues, the work of Jewish-American novelist Philip Roth foreshadows films like *American Pie*. Many of Roth's literary trademarks (especially his droll wit and themes of sexual desire and frustration) surface in vulgar teen comedies, while Merck highlights clear parallels between *American Pie* and *Portnoy's Complaint*, Roth's 1969 breakthrough novel.[3] Sparking a storm of controversy over its candid treatment of sexuality, *Portnoy's Complaint* relates the psychiatrist's couch con-fessions of Alexander Portnoy – described by Roth as 'a lust-ridden, mother-addicted young Jewish bachelor' (quoted in Saxton, 1992: 77) – who divulges in shameful detail his experience of masturbation us-ing various aids, including a piece of liver his mother later serves for the family dinner. There is, then, a clear affinity between the sexual escapades of the two Jewish characters, Alexander Portnoy and Jim Levenstein. But, whereas *Portnoy's Complaint* portrayed the experi-ence of Jewish men feeling torn between their strict family upbringing and the 1960s' promise of sexual liberation, in *American Pie* the theme is broadened to encapsulate the more general feelings of awkwardness and frustration common to adolescence.

According to film historian Nathan Abrams (2012), the Jewish dimensions to *American Pie* are indicative of broader shifts in Hollywood. During the 1990s, Abrams argues, the US film industry saw the rise of a new generation of young, Jewish screenwriters, direc-tors and actors who – in contrast to their parents and grandparents – were not immigrants and felt a greater sense of confidence and security about being Jewish in contemporary America. *American Pie*'s creative team – screenwriter Adam Herz and directors the Weitz brothers – exemplified this new generation, and, in an interview with the *Jewish Journal*, Herz related how the film's protagonist was a semi-autobiographical version of his own experience of articulating a mod-ern Jewish identity. 'In my mind', Herz explained, 'Jim, like me, is a guy who had a bar mitzvah but protested going to Sunday school'. And, while Herz recalls that his classmates' attitude to his ethnicity was ignorant, it was not expressly anti-Semitic – 'It was like, "So, you're Jewish. Have you gotten your Christmas tree yet?"' (quoted in Pfefferman, 2001).

Herz's recollections support Abrams' view that the 1990s 'new wave' of Jewish filmmakers were relatively confident in their Jewish identity. This self-assurance, moreover, was registered in their movies. 'Less anxious, less afraid of stoking an antisemitic backlash', Abrams argues, they were 'more willing to put Jews onscreen regardless of plot imperative and without feeling the need to either express or explain away their presence/absence' (2012: 12). Indeed, in the *American Pie* films, Jim Levenstein's Jewishness is relatively incidental. In fact, while listed in *American Pie*'s cast list as 'Jim Levenstein', it is only in *American Pie 2* that Jim's full name is spoken. The *Pie* movies, therefore, testify to Abrams' contention that, since 1990, Jewish identities have been 'normalised' in a growing number of films insofar as 'the addition of the Jewishness to a character, or a Jewish character, makes no major difference to the trajectory of a story, plot or narrative arc, except to insert a gag line or an "in-joke" to be read by those who understand the cultural codes' (13).[4] Moreover, while some old stereotypes still resurface in the *American Pie* series, Abrams argues the movies work to appropriate and reverse them. This is especially true of their treatment of Jewish masculinity.

Typically, Abrams suggests, mainstream films such as *Schindler's List* (Spielberg, 1994) configure Jewish masculinity in terms of humiliation and victimhood. But, Abrams contends, *American Pie*'s Jim Levenstein challenges this paradigm. In some ways, of course, Jim typifies the *schlemiel* (a Yiddish term meaning 'fool' or 'incompetent person'), a longstanding stereotype in which the Jew's body is 'represented as a site of fun, laughter and most usually ridicule' (39). *American Pie*, however, signals a representational shift. Obviously, Jim's humiliations and bodily sufferings are habitually chronicled. Significantly, however, he is never defeated and beaten. As Abrams argues, whatever life throws at the unfortunate Jim, 'he always comes out on top, emerging as the hero' (40). In the character of Jim Levenstein, therefore, the established stereotypes of Jewish victimhood resurface but, crucially, they are redefined and reversed because Jim is always presented as being – at the end of the day – cheerfully triumphant.

Increasing representations of 'sex-obsessed Jews' are also, Abrams suggests, a measure of the self-assurance felt by Hollywood's new Jewish filmmakers (73). According to Abrams, their sense of security allowed the new wave of Jewish screenwriters and directors to

appropriate and invert anti-Semitic stereotypes by developing positive depictions of lascivious Jews. The trend was anticipated by Jim's
sexual antics in *American Pie*, but it was given fuller expression in the
work of director/producer Judd Apatow and his team of collaborators
(the 'Jew Tang Clan') – especially in Apatow's production *Superbad*,
a vulgar teen comedy redolent of *Pie* in its portrayal of three Jewish
teenagers' dogged efforts to lose their virginity.

Other changes in the representation of Jewish sexuality have also
been notable. Abrams, for example, argues that *American Wedding* – the
only *Pie* movie in which Jim's Jewish heritage is explicitly highlighted –
is one among a number of movies that present a radical departure in
portrayals of Jewish femininity. In *American Wedding* this is embodied in Jim's grandmother (Angela Paton) who, Abrams suggests, 'un-
dergoes a transformation from the traditional representation of the
Jewess (as an 'ugly old kike') into a giggly lover' (87). When she first appears, Grandma Levenstein is configured as the stereotypical Jewish
matriarch, irritated that her grandson is marrying a non-Jew – after
peering closely at Michelle, Grandma cries. 'Not Jewish! No wedding,
Jimmy. No wedding. *Goyeh* [non-Jewess]!'. As the plot shifts to the wedding hotel, however, Grandma Levenstein has an amorous encounter
with Stifler who, in a darkened linen closet, mistakes the old lady for
Michelle's younger sister. But, rather than protesting, Grandma urges
Stifler to carry on – and, when the Stifmeister is distracted, she implores him to 'Focus, focus'. And, as the scene moves to the wedding
itself, Grandma Levenstein has become a picture of guilt-free hap-
piness, her anger at Jim's union assuaged by her steamy assignation.
'Look at the smile on my mother's face', Jim's Dad observes, 'Do you
know how long she's been waiting for a day like this?'.

For Abrams, such representations offer 'a transgressive eroticisa-
tion of the Jewess in contemporary cinema' (ibid.). However, while
Grandma Levenstein's accidental sex with the Stifmeister may well
challenge traditional Jewish stereotypes, the extent to which this particular 'transgression' is in any sense liberatory remains debatable.
Certainly, Mandy Merck is unimpressed and argues the scene effectively torpedoes the 'feminist' pretensions of the *American Pie* films
(2007: 273).

Bonding in the fraternal 'Dugout': the homosociality of *American Pie*

American Pie is, perhaps, more progressive in its representation of
young masculinity. Masculine identities and their male relationships

are, in fact, at the heart of the film. As screenwriter Adam Herz explains, the movie is principally about the bonds between Jim and his buddies. 'Friendship is the essential ingredient of *American Pie*', Herz has argued, 'The humor comes from the friendships we all make growing up, the people you first fall in love with, the friends who've seen you make a complete fool of yourself, the ones you hope you'll stay friends with forever' (quoted in Siegel, 2012). The point is underscored by a scene in the documentary *American Pie Revealed*, which sees Herz's school friends from East Grand Rapids reunited in Yesterdog, the local diner that was the inspiration for Dog Days (the *Pie* boys' favorite hangout). Amid laughter, Herz's old pals swap humorous reminiscences and discuss who *American Pie*'s various characters are based on. 'Well, Stifler is based on a real person who isn't here today', reveals one of Herz's former classmates. 'He's still alive, though', adds another.[5]

For David Greven, this kind of male friendship is 'the primary social model' of the vulgar teen comedies of the late 1990s and early 2000s (2002: 15). While the sexual pursuit of women is a principal interest in the lives of these films' characters, it is male camaraderie that is ultimately privileged (see Figure 5.1). In vulgar teen comedies, Greven observes, women represent 'an alien mystery that threatens to disrupt the boys' bonds', whereas male friendship is configured as 'the dugout where the boys catch their breath during the game of heterosexual conquest' (16). Indeed, in *American Pie* the importance of friendship and homosociality – that is to say, the realm of same-sex

Figure 5.1 Male camaraderie is confirmed as Jim and his buddies meet in Dog Years.

relations – is emphasised by the terms of their 'sexual pact'. 'Separately, we are flawed and vulnerable', Kevin exhorts, 'But together we are masters of our sexual destiny'

And the theme is underlined by Stifler's attempts to be accepted within the fraternal 'dugout'. While the Stifmeister always treats Jim and his buddies as hopeless inadequates, across the film series the importance of their friendship to him becomes clear. In *American Wedding*, for example, Stifler insists on organising Jim's stag-night and, when it transpires he has accidentally destroyed the wedding flowers, Stifler retrieves the situation by assembling the football team he coaches and marshalling them in the task of rebuilding the floral decorations. And Stifler's redemption seems complete when he presents Michelle's sister with a rose in an act of sincere contrition. 'Steve Stifler just gave a girl a flower and meant it', gasps a girl, 'This is awesome, it's like watching monkeys using tools for the first time'.

In *American Reunion*, however, Stifler's friendship with the others is tested. As Stifler's party descends into chaos, an exasperated Jim and his buddies ultimately admit they are fed up with Stifler's immaturity and no longer want him to organise their get-togethers. The Stifmeister is left distraught. But guilt sets in when Jim and co. visit their old high school and, looking at the senior students' 'wish list' recorded on the wall, they see that Stifler's big hope was 'to keep the party going with my boys'. Remorseful, they find Stifler at work and make amends – prompting a revitalized Stifler to stand up for himself by thoroughly humiliating his obnoxious boss. Then, at the reunion, the friendship is restored further. Jim and the others apologize to Stifler and, insisting he is their friend, they admit that high school would have been no fun without him. The bonds of male friendship, therefore, are resolutely re-affirmed.

At the same time, however, there are distinct parameters to this homosociality. As Greven argues, constructions of masculinity in teen comedies are characterised by a pronounced sense of anxiety and a simultaneous fascination and repulsion with homosexuality. While neither *American Pie* nor its immediate sequel have any explicitly gay characters, Greven suggests that 'a recognition of a pervasive gay threat to conventional masculinity permeates both films' (2002: 19). In the original movie the theme surfaces in Stifler's use of the word 'gay' as a casual insult, and in the way he is pole-axed by revulsion when he realises he has drunk Kevin's semen-tainted beer. But it becomes more pronounced in *American Pie 2* as Stifler, Greven contends, 'becomes the battleground for the films' warring impulses between interest in homoeroticism and revulsion from it' (ibid.).

This is especially evident in one of *American Pie 2*'s key scenes. During the summer vacation Jim and the gang find work in Grand Harbor painting a house whose residents are two young, attractive women. Ever the crass thickhead, Stifler suspects the girls are lesbians and decides to search the house for evidence. After searching high and low, Stifler finally stumbles across what he assumes is indelible proof. With near apoplectic glee he holds aloft what he takes to be a 'lesbian artifact', then charges around the house elatedly, shouting:

> Holy shit, dude, I found a dildo! [manic laughter] Big blue rubber dicks for everyone! The people demand rubber dicks! Dildo! Dildo! Dildo!

When the girls suddenly return, however, they catch Jim, Finch and Stifler hiding in their bedroom. But, instead of calling the cops, they turn the tables on the intruders. Taking mischievous revenge for the boys' chauvinist presumptions, the girls offer to perform 'lesbian sex' in exchange for a similar homosexual performance from the guys. For every fake lesbian kiss and caress, the girls demand corresponding acts from the trio. Despite the humiliation, the fantasy of lesbian titillation proves too much to resist and the boys initially comply. Yet, as things get increasingly risqué, Jim and Finch get more reticent. In contrast, Stifler remains eager – even when the girls offer to take their 'lesbian' act further if the guys first go down on one another. Stifler stays animatedly willing, but for Jim and Finch it is the last straw and they flee, shrieking. The scene, then, drips with anxious homoeroticism and, as Greven, observes, its conclusion seems to 'suggest the movie's hurried determination to reestablish the essentially disgusting nature of gay sex' (2002: 19). Indeed, later in the film, heterosexual horizons are firmly reinstated at a party where a delighted Stifler finally scores a threesome with the two 'lesbians'.

There is, then, a clear whiff of homophobia in the *American Pie* movies. But, as so often with the *Pie* films, the treatment of homosexuality is ambivalent. In the case of *American Pie 2*'s 'lesbian scene', for example, shrill anxiety surrounds the boy's 'gay' performance, but, as Greven argues, 'the sheer length of the scene implies an interest in pushing past the borders of straight male sexual taste' (19). And in *American Wedding*, Roz Kaveney notes, there is 'the mild frisson of sexual ambiguity' in a scene where Stifler teaches Jim to dance (2006: 151). Later in the movie this is played out further as the boys mistakenly find themselves in a Chicago gay bar. Stifler causes endless offence but, just as he and the others are to be unceremoniously ejected, the Stifmeister challenges an angry patron – the huge, bearded 'Bear' – to a dance-off. The wild duets that ensue are hilarious but, as Kaveney observes, the friendship that develops between the two characters is more significant in the way it suggests 'an intimacy that transcends sex' (ibid.).

American Reunion, moreover, sees a series of disclosures that seem like revelatory punch-lines to sexual 'in-jokes' running throughout the film series. Jessica, for instance, reveals she is a lesbian and introduces her girlfriend, Ingrid. And, at Stifler's party, hugs and manly banter ensue as two of his old sports buddies arrive. 'Hey, what have you two cock-smokers been up to?', Stifler jovially enquires. 'Well, we just got engaged', one replies, while the other proudly holds up a hand to show an engagement ring. Stunned, Stifler laughs incredulously, 'What?! That's so fucking gay'. But the joke is on him. 'Yeah Stifler, we *are* gay', one responds. 'Half the lacrosse team was gay', elaborates the other, 'You *must* have known that. You walked in on Doug and Barry when they were in the showers'. Stifler blinks in bewilderment, and thinks back – 'I just thought they were wrestling…'. By the end of the movie, however, Stifler's homophobic prejudices are shrugged away as the gay teammates ask him to plan their wedding. 'I'd love to', affirms the Stifmeister happily – though he still looks decidedly awkward as he is sandwiched between the two in a mighty cuddle.

The most intriguing revelation, however, relates to the MILF Guys. At Stifler's party John Cho's character wanders in. Slightly effete (he notices Michelle's change of hair tint), he is conspicuously alone. 'So, is your buddy, the other MILF Guy, here tonight?', asks Jim, 'I thought you always came to these things together?'. 'Let's just say', Cho's character forlornly replies, 'that friendship is a…two-way street.' The audience is left wondering, but a further teaser comes as the party crowd watches a video clip of Oz dancing in a *Celebrity Dance-Off* TV show. Noticing Oz's muscular physique, Cho's character enthuses, 'Dude, you have an amazing body'. By the end of the movie, however, Cho's MILF Guy is still alone. Sitting, dejectedly, at night in the high school football stadium, he sips sadly from a beer bottle. But then the mood lifts as the other MILF Guy suddenly appears. Spotting each other, they call out like mating birds. 'MILF?', queries one. 'MILF!', the other responds emphatically, and the two blissfully embrace. The audience, however, never quite know the reality of the MILF Guys' relationship. Like so much in the *American Pie* movies, the issue is left fairly open-ended.

'I'm Steve Stifler, and I Have an Eleven-Inch Penis': models of masculinity in *American Pie*

The intricacies of male relationships in the *American Pie* films testify to changing constructions of masculinity during the 1990s and 2000s. The work of R.W. Connell has been especially influential in highlighting the shifts. Drawing attention to the way notions of masculinity are socially and culturally constructed, Connell demonstrates the way issues of class, 'race' and sexuality shape 'multiple masculinities' that are structured in a hierarchy of dominance and subordination (1995: 75–8). For Connell, in contemporary American culture, the most dominant, socially endorsed form of masculinity – or 'hegemonic masculinity' – is associated with characteristics such as aggressiveness, strength, drive, ambition, lack of emotion and self-reliance. This hegemonic masculinity, moreover, is primarily constituted through the subordination of women and other forms of masculinity, in particular the effeminacy associated with male homosexuality (78–9).

At the same time, however, Connell argues that hegemonic masculinity is always open to challenges from alternative versions of masculine identity. He identifies, for example, a 'new age' form of masculinity that was informed by the ideas of feminism and, as a consequence was supportive to women, was critical of chauvinism and was comfortable with displays of sensitivity and emotional depth (120–42). And, throughout the 1990s, many theorists argued that feminism, gay liberation and (especially) an explosion of male consumerism were increasingly working to challenge hegemonic forms of masculinity. Mark Simpson (1994), for instance, highlighted the way traditional understandings of masculinity centred on work and formal public life were giving way to media- and image-driven forms of masculine identity configured around appearance and narcissism, and that this, in turn, was working to blur boundaries between 'gay' and 'straight' sexual identities. Released in 1999, *American Pie* both reflected and was itself constituent in such developments. As Sharyn Pearce observes, *Pie*'s creative team 'appear to have been keenly aware of contemporary changes in the cultural prescriptions of gender, of the fragile, provisional and unstable makeup of masculinity and its many transient, unfinished, and incomplete guises' (2003: 78). In this respect *American Pie* epitomised the more general changes in Hollywood's treatment of masculinity during the 1990s and 2000s.

For film theorist Susan Jeffords, US films of the 1980s were dominated by spectacular images of white, male action heroes. According to Jeffords, the 'hard-bodied' action heroes of 1980s blockbuster movies such as *Rambo: First Blood, Part 2* (Cosmatos, 1985), *Lethal Weapon* (Donner, 1987) and *Die Hard* (McTiernan, 1988) represented a recuperation of militaristic ideals of masculinity in the wake of the debacle of the Vietnam War and the challenge of feminism. They also, she argues, worked to reinforce the right-wing policies of Ronald Reagan's presidency by promoting the American 'hard body' as the solution to the nation's foreign and domestic problems (Jeffords, 1989: 16–17).

With the social, cultural and political shifts of the 1990s, however, Hollywood's representations of masculinity began to change. In place of spectacles of male violence and power, there was a move to more emotional displays of masculine sensitivity and vulnerability. It was a change that registered noticeably in the world of teen cinema.

Even during the 1980s there were teen movies whose characters diverged from 'hegemonic' models of masculinity. A stock archetype, for example, was the 'nerd' character, defined by Christine Quail as 'an awkward, math-savvy social and sexual failure' who is often juxtaposed with the athletic, socially skilled and sexually aware 'cool kid' or 'jock' (2011: 460–1). The nerd became increasingly prevalent, even valorized, across popular culture, but, as Lori Kendall argues, he did not necessarily represent an unqualified challenge to hegemonic masculine ideals. The 1980s teen comedy *Revenge of the Nerds*, for example, sees a group of downtrodden nerds form a campus fraternity to take revenge on their jock nemeses – but, in so doing, the nerds effectively reproduce the same 'hypermasculinity' as their rivals. 'Nerd imagery', Kendall concludes, 'can thus either challenge or reinforce hegemonic masculinity...[and it] sometimes does both at the same time' (1999: 279). The teen movies of the late 1990s, however, saw the appearance of different models of 'non-hegemonic' masculinity. These had more in common with Connell's 'new age' masculine identity, with its dimensions of emotionality and rejection of macho chauvinism. And the characters in *American Pie* exemplify the trend.

As Pearce argues, the key protagonists in *American Pie* put a 'new millennium spin' on models of teen masculinity. 'Mostly sweet and lovable', she argues, they 'clearly develop into "new age" prototypes who are significantly molded by the women about them' (2003: 77). Indeed, for Pearce, it is the relationships Jim and his friends have with women that form the film's central theme. *'American Pie'*, she contends, 'is not ultimately about bonding with other males, or about buddies – it is much more about the defining of a male in terms of how he relates to and empathizes with women' (76). In these terms, *American Pie* constructs a form of 'feminized' masculinity, a model of manhood that develops a greater sense of empathy and emotional depth through its interaction with women. As Pearce puts it:

> In the eternal rites of passage from boy to man, and from innocence to experience, this text is principally about the construction of 'feminized' men who are more responsive to interpersonal relationships than the hegenomic norm.
>
> (ibid.)

Jim's ever-loyal dad – Noah Levenstein – also affects a masculine identity very different to the hegemonic model. Played by veteran comic actor Eugene Levy, Noah is achingly square, with his big eyebrows, round spectacles, collar and tie (even at home) and belted slacks hitched above his waist. But he is a long way from being a hidebound patriarch. Instead, he exudes a genial warmth in his blundering attempts to give succor to his disaster-prone son – qualities that Levy, himself, injected into the role. As screenwriter Herz explains:

> I had originally envisioned [the character] as a stereotypical gruff, 1950s dad.... But Eugene came in and gave him this bewildered, goofball quality. And the first time you see him and Jason [Biggs] together as father and son, you think, 'My God, that's the kind of father Jim would have to have to turn out the way he did'.
>
> (quoted in Siegel, 2012)

The theme of masculine identities that diverge from the hegemonic norm is underscored by *American Pie*'s soundtrack. Reprised throughout *Pie*'s theatrical releases, the movie's opening song – 'Laid' by indie guitar rockers James – is an especially fitting addition. The song's risqué lyrics ('This bed is on fire with passionate love...but she only comes when she's on top') obviously resonate with *American Pie*'s lewd inclinations. But the song's emotional expressivity also points towards the film's sensitive, 'feminized' forms of masculine identity ('Dress me up in women's clothes, messed around with gender roles'). And the connotations are accentuated by the way singer Tim Booth's voice goes into a high falsetto at several points in the song.

Other music also echoes the theme. The scores of the *American Pie* films are relatively eclectic, but skate-punk and pop-punk bands have a strong presence, most notably Third Eye Blind, Goldfinger, Sum 41, Alien Ant Farm, American Hi-Fi and Blink-182. Fast and furious, their songs retain the speed and attitude of classic punk rock, but they eschew conventional models of rock machismo through their melodic guitar riffs, earnest vocal styles and lyrical themes that are suffused with flip 'frat boy' humour but also evoke a sense of angst and vulnerability that fits neatly with the kind of masculinity embodied in the main *Pie* characters. Blink-182 even makes a cameo appearance in the original *American Pie*, appearing as the rock band gathered around a rehearsal studio's computer screen to watch Jim's ill-fated attempt to seduce Nadia.[6]

But hegemonic masculinity is also conspicuous in *American Pie*. Crucially, however, it is invariably a subject of ridicule. The characters

Chuck Sherman and (especially) Steve Stifler aspire to the qualities revered in hegemonic masculinity, but they are configured as figures of fun, the absurdity of their 'macho' pretensions underlined by their childish attempts to aggrandise themselves through self-invented nicknames – 'The Shermanator' and 'The Stifmeister'. And Stifler's surname, itself, does much the same. 'Stif' obviously alludes to phallic power. But the addition of the suffix 'ler' deflates these associations by introducing overtones that seem somehow unpleasant and irritating. Stifler's lecherous machinations, moreover, consistently end in ignominious failure, and he is regularly the butt of the gross-out gags. In contrast to Jim's anxious hypersensitivity, Stifler is assertive and confident, but this assuredness is portrayed as supercilious arrogance. Indeed, much of the film's humour comes from the way Stifler is portrayed as a grotesque, over-the-top caricature of hegemonic masculinity – boorish, sexist and exhibiting a staggering lack of self-awareness. It is a quality exemplified, perhaps above all, in Stifler's infantile sexual boasts. *American Reunion*, for example, sees a typical Stifler vignette. As his party hots up, a horny Stifmeister sidles up to two attractive girls and introduces himself with his characteristic air of exaggerated braggadocio. 'Ladies, I'm Steve Stifler and I have an eleven-inch penis', he grins. And, forming a large circle with both hands, the Stifmeister emphasises his prowess with laughable boastfulness – *'Around!* Think about it...'.

American Pie and the 'Mood of Nostalgia'

American Pie is set in a contemporary America, but its portrayal of US youth culture at the turn of the millennium has a distinctly 'retro' feel. The quality is intentional. The movie's production steered clear of obviously 'modern' film techniques, so conspicuous Steadicam shots, swish pans and comedic sound effects were all avoided. As director Paul Weitz explains, 'We wanted not to use a Steadicam too much because we wanted the movie to have a bit of a retro feel. Basically, we tried not to use too much technology'.[7] The use of James' 'Laid' as the movie's theme song is also quite retro. While *American Pie* was released in 1999, 'Laid' was a hit on US college radio in 1993. More than appealing to teens of the day, then, the choice of theme song for *American Pie* harked back nostalgically to the college days of the film's creators.

For Timothy Shary, a nostalgic tinge to youth films is almost unavoidable. As he points out, while teen movies may be targeted at a youth audience, they are not produced by young people themselves and so are inevitably 'filtered through an adult lens' (Shary, 2014: 2). Other commentators, however, have seen the nostalgic ambience of modern youth films as constituent in more deep-rooted cultural trends. Most famously, Frederic Jameson has argued that 'nostalgic' movies are indicative of a regrettable slide into an era of shallow postmodernism. Focusing on *American Graffiti* (George Lucas' 1973 recreation of the Californian youth culture of 1962), Jameson argues that the movie inaugurated '[a] new aesthetic discourse' – the 'nostalgia film' – which was intrinsically conservative in the way it represented the past through superficial stereotypes rather than engaging with history in any meaningful way. From this perspective, 'nostalgia films' like *American Graffiti* 'render the "past" through stylistic connotation, conveying "pastness" by the glossy qualities of the image' (Jameson, 1991: 19). According to Jameson, then, while modernist forms of art once provided audiences with a meaningful access to history, the postmodern 'nostalgia film' recalls nothing more than a superficial impression of the past through an aesthetic style dominated by fashion, style and surface.

It is, perhaps, unlikely that Jameson has ever seen any of the *American Pie* movies. But, if he did so, the venerable theorist might find qualities that appear to support his critique. The films, for example, can be seen as representing a 'postmodern' recycling of the recent past in the way they mimic the vulgar teen comedies of the 1980s, reproducing their gross-out style for a new generation. The *Pie* movies are also replete with postmodern-*esque* quotations and intertextual references. *American Pie*, for example, clearly alludes to 1985's *The Breakfast Club* when Simple Minds' 'Don't You Forget About Me' is played in its prom scene (in reality it would have been an unlikely choice for a 1999 prom). And there are obvious references to *The Graduate* (Nichols, 1967) as Finch meets Stifler's Mom at the post-prom party and, in a witty piece of gender-reversal, she asks, 'Mr. Finch, are you trying to seduce me?', while Simon and Garfunkel's 'Mrs. Robinson' plays in the background.

The setting for *American Pie*, too, seems to evoke 'a superficial impression of the past'. The film was shot in California, using Universal's sound stages and location shoots in various Long Beach high schools and private residences in the San Fernando Valley. The movie, however, is purposefully set in Michigan (with East Great Falls standing in for East Grand Rapids, the town of Adam Herz's youth). As a consequence, location filming saw teams of technicians carefully revamp the school corridors (even repainting student lockers) to create more of a 'Midwestern' look, while outdoor shots carefully avoided palm trees or the Spanish, mission-style architecture typical of Southern California. The effect is to create a stylized, 'glossy' ideal of Midwestern school days, with the film seeming to be set in an eerily timeless Middle America.

Jameson's ideas about the 'postmodern' qualities of contemporary culture have, however, attracted strong criticism. Notably, Linda Hutcheon (1989) contests the assumption that there can be any engagement with an 'authentic' history existing outside its cultural referents. As she explains, 'there is no directly and accessible past "real" for us today: we can only know – and construct – the past through its traces, its representations' (Hutcheon, 1989: 109). And, more importantly for *American Pie*, the use of nostalgia and historical allusion often amount to much more than what Jameson would dismiss as a shallow attempt to 'imitate dead styles' (Jameson, 1985: 114). As John Storey (2001) argues, the re-animation of historical aesthetics is a practice of active cultural enterprise in which media forms of the past are commandeered and employed in meaningful ways in the lived cultures of the present (Storey, 2001: 247). In these terms, *American Pie* may plunder from the styles and aesthetics of teen films from the past, but it remains a text firmly rooted in its own historical context, and its representations of youth, gender and sexuality relate to the distinctive identities and experiences of young people during the late 1990s and 2000s.

There is, though, another sense in which the *American Pie* films are nostalgic. For Paul Grainge, an important distinction can be made between the *mode* of nostalgia and the *mood* of nostalgia. While the nostalgic mode is manifest in the kind of historical imitation criticised by Jameson, the nostalgic mood is an emotional state characterised by a yearning for the past (Grainge, 2000: 28). The nostalgic mood, then, constitutes a form of 'idealized remembrance' which results from – and further contributes to – an idealisation of the past (ibid.). And the *American Pie* series has a distinct 'mood of nostalgia'. The original movie, for instance, concludes on a note of definite melancholy. Following Stifler's post-prom party Jim and his buddies are assembled in Dog Days. They are cheerful, but their toast 'To the next step...' has a discernible bitter-sweet tinge. They are hopeful for the future, but they also seem reflective and wistful as they face the end of an era (see Figure 5.2).

The *Pie* boys' adventures were revived in the following two movies, but after *American Wedding*, screenwriter Herz announced it was time to end the fun. 'There won't be another one', he explained in an interview, 'Simply because I don't have any stories left to tell about these guys' (quoted in Otto, 2003). Nevertheless, thirteen years after the original movie, the gang returned in 2012's *American Reunion*. The *Pie* series, then, became virtually unique in the world of teen cinema

Figure 5.2 'To the next step...' – Finch (Eddie Kaye Thomas) and Oz (Chris Klein) ponder the end of an era.

in its ability to trace its characters' lives and relationships through the process of ageing.[8] And, while the film retains the gross-out trademarks of its predecessors, its nostalgic elements are more pronounced. Now in their early thirties, the *Pie* characters are all somewhat regretful about their lives and seem to hanker after their halcyon high school days. Not least Stifler, who struggles uncomprehendingly with the expectations of adulthood. Bouncing into his party, the Stifmeister is still his usual self, but intervening time has left him an anachronism. Wearing a tee-shirt whose slogan proudly proclaims its wearer an 'Orgasm Donor', Stifler stares in astonishment at the other partygoers. Demurely dressed for a mature evening, the couples nibble hors d'oeuvres and sip glasses of wine. 'What the fuck is this?!', screeches a stunned Stifler. And, noticing the soft tune playing quietly in the background, he stammers, 'Who the hell changed the music?'. 'Sorry', a young mother apologises. And, as her partner coddles their tiny infant, she explains, 'We thought this was more baby-friendly'. Mortified, Stifler throws his hands up, aghast at the way things have changed.

A mood of nostalgia, then, snakes through the *American Pie* narrative. The films celebrate a rose-tinted adolescence of carefree fun and friendship, but they also point to the transience and ephemeral nature of youth. Indeed, these are qualities hinted at in the choice of title. Young men's quest to lose their virginity may well be 'as American as apple pie', but the film title's reference to Don McLean's 1971 folk-rock anthem also taps into a rich vein of melancholy. While McLean was always reluctant to explain the symbolism of 'American Pie', the song has been widely interpreted as a morose look back at America's loss of innocence amid the social and political turmoil of the 1960s.[9] And, while the song itself never features in any of the *American Pie* movies, hints of its 'end of an era' melancholia undoubtedly surface.

Like all youth movies, then, *American Pie* and its sequels are distinguished by their particular construction of young people and youth culture. 'Coming-of-age' and the transition to adulthood are experiences invariably central to youth films, and *American Pie* is significant for the way it marked a shift in the treatment of these themes. The movie is certainly more sexually explicit than its predecessors, but, along with this, it also places much greater stress on the role of personal relationships and the acquisition of emotional empathy in the move from youth to adulthood. Together with other youth movies, *American Pie* is also characterised by particular configurations of youth in terms of class, ethnicity and gender. And, while its representations of class and ethnicity might be regarded as relatively conservative, *American Pie*'s construction of gender – especially masculinity – is more progressive, articulating new models of masculine identity characterised by more pronounced dimensions of sensitivity and vulnerability. At the same time, however, these elements remain framed within an overarching mood of nostalgia that points to the transience and ephemeral nature of youth – qualities that continue to surface in the more recent entries in the canon of vulgar teen comedy.

Notes

1 In her influential (1992) analysis of 1980s 'slasher' movies, Clover argues these films were distinctly misogynist in their treatment of teen sexuality. Nowell (2011), however, suggests their sexual politics were often more nuanced than many critics have acknowledged.

2 Weitz and Hertz discuss the film's prom scene in the audio commentary included as a bonus feature on the 2001 DVD release of *American Pie*.

3 In 1972 *Portnoy's Complaint* was, itself, released as film comedy written and directed by Ernest Lehman.

4 While this trait may have become more common in movies of the 1990s, earlier examples certainly exist. In *Dirty Dancing* (Ardolino, 1987), for instance, the Jewishness of the central character – Frances 'Baby' Houseman (Jennifer Grey) – is largely incidental to the film's plot.

5 See *American Pie Revealed* (2003). In 2011 a Florida newspaper claimed the individual who had been the inspiration for Steve Stifler had been arrested after a stabbing in a barroom brawl. Subsequently, he was convicted of second-degree murder. Speaking to a reporter, however, screenwriter Herz did not confirm the connection. Explaining that Stifler was a composite character based on several people he had known in high school, Herz added, ' It's not something I feel comfortable talking about' (Barton, 2011).

6 At the time Blink-182 had just completed their breakthrough album, *Enema of the State,* and the band were cast in the movie when guitarist Tom Delonge's acting agent heard a band was needed for the brief scene.

7 Weitz's account appears in the audio commentary available on the *American Pie* 2001 DVD release.

8 The only other movie to attempt something similar is *Boyhood* (2014), Richard Linklater's coming-of-age epic, that was filmed between 2001 and 2013 and tracks the childhood and adolescence of Mason Evans Jr. (Ellar Coltrane) as he grows up in Texas with his divorced parents (Patricia Arquette and Ethan Hawke).

9 In 2015, however, McLean finally broke his silence. As the original manuscript for his song's lyrics was auctioned (for $1.2 million), McLean told reporters – 'Basically in "American Pie", things are heading in the wrong direction. ... It is becoming less idyllic. I don't know whether you consider that wrong or right, but it is a morality song in a sense' (quoted in Moyer, 2015).

6 Vulgar teen comedy
The last crumbs

New directions for the vulgar teen comedy

For modern-day audiences, the vulgar teen comedies of the past can seem like antiquated time capsules. Campaigns such as 2017's #MeToo Movement, and similar large-scale protests against sexual harassment, signpost the way views on gender, ethnicity and sexuality have changed. In this context, many teen comedies from the 1970s, 1980s, 1990s and even 2000s can now seem not just dated but decidedly offensive in terms of their stereotypes and attitudes. Writing in 2014, for instance, film critic Robbie Collin observed how 1978's *National Lampoon's Animal House* seemed to have aged badly. 'It's hard to imagine', Collin wrote, 'a film being made today in which one of the heroes amusingly wrestles with his conscience over whether or not he should take advantage of a thirteen-year-old girl who has passed out naked on a friend's bed' (Collin, 2014). Other, more execrable, examples also stand out. In its tale of three college boys who dress as women in order to infiltrate a sorority house, *Sorority Boys* (Wolodarsky, 2002) demonstrates levels of misogyny that are hard to stomach. And the racial politics of *Soul Man* (Miner, 1986) – the story of a young, white guy who takes suntan pills so he can pass as black, thereby qualifying for a black-only scholarship at Harvard – now seem to defy belief.

The *American Pie* series – the theatrically released movies, at least – are less guilty. Indeed, in their relatively (for the time) progressive treatment of young masculinities and femininities, the *Pie* films testify to the way social attitudes to gender and sexuality took steps forward during the late 1990s and 2000s. Nevertheless, as a new generation watch the comedies of yesteryear on streaming services such as Netflix, some young audiences are still taken aback by the *Pie* movies' treatment of sex and gender. Voicing their criticisms on Twitter, for example, one young viewer complained, 'American pie is such a cliché dumbass sexist movie why is it on my tv' [sic.], while another averred that *American Pie* 'is the dumbest and most sexist movie ever' (quoted in Taylor, 2018).

Shifting attitudes to sexuality and representations of gender may, in some part, account for the waning popularity of the vulgar teen comedy after the 2000s. Following the success of the first *American Pie* movies, there had ensued a torrent of teen comedy releases but, as the millennium progressed, their numbers fizzled. Beyond shifts in social attitudes, however, other factors may also have played a part in the decline. As Michael Pokorny and his associates show, since the 1990s, Hollywood has taken a more conservative approach to film-making in terms of funneling a greater proportion of film budgets into G-, PG- or PG13-rated releases. While such movies accounted for just 50% of film budgets during the early 1990s, the figure had grown to 80% by the mid-2010s (Pokorny et al., 2019: 33). This shift of invest-ment into films geared to an 'all ages' audience will obviously have militated against the production of gross-out movies given the intrin-sically risqué nature of their humour. Consequently, while successful gross-out comedies were still released, by the end of the 2010s, their numbers seemed to have thinned. Many of the those that appeared, moreover, tended to blend 'gross-out' elements within a revived ver-sion of the romantic comedy, and usually focused on the relationships of adults rather than teenagers – exemplified most obviously by the Judd Apatow production, *Bridesmaids* (Feig, 2011).

Indeed, the increasing role of adults in gross-out-*esque* movies was a distinct trend of the 2000s. Of course, adults had often appeared in the early vulgar teen comedies. Adult characters were central, for example, in several notable vulgar comedies geared to a youth audi-ence. *Caddyshack* (Ramis, 1980) stands out in this respect, as does the *National Lampoon* 'Vacation' series penned by John Hughes and star-ring Chevy Chase as the calamity-prone family man, Clark Griswold.[1] During the 2000s, however, it became more common for adults rather than teens to feature in gross-out themed pictures. Clearly, *American Wedding* and *American Reunion* were part of the trend, but the roster also included *Old School*, *Wedding Crashers* (Dobkin, 2005), *Step Brothers* (McKay, 2008), *The Hangover* (Philips, 2009), Phil Lord and Christopher Miller's *21 Jump Street* (2012) and its sequel *22 Jump Street* (2014), along with Judd Apatow's *The 40-Year-Old Virgin* (2005), *Knocked Up* (2007) and *Funny People* (2009).

This proliferation of movies informed by the codes and conventions of vulgar teen comedy, but featuring adult characters and aimed at a cross-generational (rather than specifically teenage) audience, was rooted in wider cultural shifts. In the early twenty-first century the boundaries of 'youth culture' became more blurred, and distinctions between 'youth' and 'adulthood' became increasingly hazy. The change was partly indebted to transformations of labour markets, educational provision and family structure which effectively extended 'youth' as a life-stage – a development indicated by lengthened careers in education, later entry into full-time employment and rises in mean ages of first marriages and births to women. For theorists such as American sociologist Jeffrey Arnett (2004), these changes had even spawned a new, distinctive period in the life-course – 'emergent adulthood' – a phase when individuals 'paused' their social development to enjoy a prolonged youth so that, for Arnett, adulthood did not begin much before the age of thirty.[2] Perhaps more significant, however, was the degree to which 'youthful' tastes and attitudes increasingly featured in the way older age groups constructed and expressed their identities.

The shift was highlighted by commentators such as Christopher Noxon who, in 2006, coined the term 'rejuvenile' for what he saw as 'a new breed of adult, identified by a determination to remain playful, energetic, and flexible in the face of adult responsibilities' (Noxon, 2006: 2). And commercial interests were quick to latch onto the lucrative potential of protracted 'youth'. The market research agency Viacom Brand Solutions International, for example, trumpeted a new market of adult consumers who were still actively and emotionally connected to youth culture. As their 2008 report, *The Golden Age of Youth*, advised:

> The traditional demographic definition of 'youth' is no longer applicable in today's society, and marketers should target consumers based upon their engagement and participation with youth culture rather than their chronological age.
>
> (Viacom Brand Solutions International, 2008: 1)

It was these kind of economic and cultural shifts, then, that generated the market for the new wave of movies that were rooted in the traditions of the vulgar teen comedy, but which featured adult characters and were geared to cross-generational audiences. Youth-focused versions of the vulgar teen comedy, however, also still survived. But, while the 'classic' template remained influential, the newer vulgar teen movies evidenced significant change and development. Beyond the US, for example, distinctly local versions of the format began to surface.

As Timothy Shary argues, outside Hollywood, adolescence and youth have been a common subject in cinema around the world. Many international youth films, moreover, deal with topics generally down-played in US teen movies – for example, politics, religion and tensions around cultural and national identity (Shary, 2007: 4). International teen comedies, however, have been relatively rare. And *vulgar* teen comedies especially so. This is, perhaps, because gross-out humour has peculiarly national roots. As film theorist Alan Williams contends, 'Whatever one thinks of "gross-out" comedies they are, doubt-less, typically "American"' (Williams, 2002: 18). This is not to say that other countries do not possess their own traditions of 'carnivalesque' vulgarity. In Britain, for instance, cultural historian Andy Medhurst shows how a long tradition of lewd and bawdy humour stretches from the nineteenth-century music hall to the long-running *Carry On...* series of films released during the 1960s and 1970s (Medhurst, 1986). But it was only in the 2000s that something recognisable as a British vulgar teen comedy appeared in the form of *Kevin and Perry Go Large* (Bye, 2000). Based on characters developed by comedian Harry Enfield on his TV sketch show, the film features Enfield and Kathy Burke as two 15-year-old boys – the spotty and precocious Kevin (Enfield) and his monumentally hopeless best friend Perry (Burke)[3] – who travel to Ibiza in a desperate quest to both lose their virginity and make it big as dance music DJs. The movie's coming-of-age themes and ribald hu-mour were clearly indebted to the period's cycle of American vulgar teen comedies, an influence that was also clear in *The Inbetweeners*.

The Inbetweeners began life as a sitcom, originally appearing on the British TV channel E4 and airing between 2008 and 2010. Created and written by Damon Beesley and Ian Morris, the show followed the mis-adventures of suburban teenager Will (Simon Bird) and his friends Simon (Joe Thomas), Neil (Blake Harrison) and Jay (James Buckley) at the fictional Rudge Park Comprehensive School. The series ob-viously drew inspiration from the likes of the *American Pie* movies through its focus on the vagaries of male friendship, combined with a humour based on gross-out jokes and the gormless yet endearing foursome's (usually foundering) bids for sexual experience. And, after becoming a TV hit, the show spawned its own big screen spin-offs. In *The Inbetweeners Movie* (Palmer, 2011), the boys' final year of school is over and they head to Crete in search of sun, sea and (as Jay indeli-cately puts it) 'wall-to-wall clunge'. Subsequently, *The Inbetweeners 2* (Beesley and Morris, 2014) finds the friends backpacking in Australia as they try to rekindle the hedonistic excitement of their schooldays. *The Inbetweeners*, then, plainly owed a debt to US traditions of vulgar teen comedy, but the British incarnation is not simply a straightfor-ward imitation of the American original. Instead, a distinctly 'British' spin is put on the formula. Elements of irony, for example, are played more heavily. And, more importantly, *The Inbetweeners* foregrounds issues of social class much more than its US equivalents.[4] Indeed, much of *The Inbetweeners'* humour arises from the way a change in family circumstances has forced the upper middle-class, privately-educated Will into an expedient friendship with his more downscale buddies.

Issues of social class, in contrast, remained resolutely invisible in America's more recent vulgar teen comedies. Greater change, however, registered in the realms of ethnicity, gender and sexuality. For instance, the successful *Harold & Kumar* movie series featured the goofy antics of two Asian-American stoners, Harold Lee (a Korean-American, played by John Cho – *American Pie*'s MILF Guy # 2) and Kumar Patal (an Indian-American, played by Kal Penn).[5] Greater diversity in terms of gender and sexuality, meanwhile, also featured in a flurry of female-oriented movies produced in the vein of vulgar teen comedies. For instance, Kay Cannon's directorial debut, *Blockers* (2018), relates the efforts of a trio of parents to stop their daughters from losing their virginity on prom night. The movie revisits many of the familiar tropes of the vulgar teen comedy – steadfast friendships, the coming-of-age sexual pact, the high school prom as a rite-of-passage landmark, together with an assortment of gross-out touches (including an extended projectile-vomiting sequence). Significantly, however, *Blockers* inverts the usual blueprint by focusing on the sexual pact of three girls – Julie (Kathryn Newton), Kayla (Geraldine Viswanathan) and Sam (Gideon Adlon) – who are all configured as strong, intelligent and independent. And *Blockers'* 'feminist' proclivities are underscored by Kayla's pointedly levelheaded mom (Sarayu Blue), who makes a fiery speech about sexual double standards and the misguided politics of policing girls' sexuality. Clearly, this is not something that would have happened in *Porky's*. At the same time, however, *Blockers* can seem a bit slow and pedestrian. And the movie is as much about the angst-ridden parents as it is about the kids, albeit with a twist that one father is concerned his gay daughter will relent to heterosexist expectations by having sex with her (male) prom date.

A sharper and more refreshing updating of the vulgar teen comedy appears in *Booksmart* (2019). The directorial debut for actor-turned-filmmaker Olivia Wilde, *Booksmart* centres on dorky best friends Molly (Beanie Feldstein) and Amy (Kaitlyn Dever). Academic over-achievers, they have spent their school careers single-mindedly focused on their studies. Earnest and industrious, they have fake IDs, but only so they can get into the library at night, and their secret code-word is 'Malala' (as in Yousafzai, the young Pakistani activist). Molly is headed for Yale University and a highflying political career, while Amy will spend the summer 'in Botswana helping women make their own tampons' before attending Columbia. On the eve of graduation, however, the pair suddenly realise they have missed out on years of teenage fun. So, determined to make up for lost time, the friends decide to cram four years' worth of adventure into one night of hard partying.[6] The film's take on gender and sexuality is bold and progressive, but, as it was originally formulated, the movie was more conservative. Written by Emily Halpern and Sarah Haskins, the movie's initial screenplay was first touted around Hollywood in 2009, and its précis outlined a version of the vulgar teen comedy that, despite a gender-twist, was fairly traditional:

> Two overachieving high school seniors realize the only thing they haven't accomplished is having boyfriends, and each resolves to find one by prom.
>
> (quoted in Guerrascio, 2019)

A long period of pre-production, however, saw the movie overhauled. Most importantly, Susanna Fogel revised the screenplay in 2014 and – significantly – rewrote one lead character (Amy) as a lesbian and modified the story so the friends are not solely fixated on a quest for boyfriends. Instead, while both girls have sights set on their respective crushes, the friends are also determined to have a blast together before moving on with their lives. In these terms, then, the rewritten (and ultimately released) version of *Booksmart* can be seen as reconfiguring the traditions of the vulgar teen comedy, effectively updating and reformulating its conventions in a way that addressed contemporary shifts in cultural attitudes and outlooks – much as *American Pie* had done, in its own way, twenty years earlier.

'To the Next Step…'?

American Pie, meanwhile, had not completely disappeared. After the release of *American Reunion* in 2012 Universal hired the movie's writer/ director team of Jon Hurwitz and Hayden Schlossberg to write a further sequel. Provisionally titled *American Pie 5*, the screenplay was duly completed, purportedly with a plot that sees Jim Levenstein and his buddies beset by embarrassing misfortune as they vacation in Las Vegas. However, following *American Reunion*'s relatively disappointing performance at the US Box Office, the sequel's script stayed on the shelf. Nevertheless, interest in another *Pie* movie remained high, actor

Seann William Scott speculating that, 'It could still be really funny to see Stifler as this sad, male stripper just dancing for dollar bills' (quoted in Chase, 2018). At the time of writing (2019) rumours of another slice of *American Pie* continue to circulate, but there is nothing firmly in the oven. Yet the door remains open for additional servings. Following on from *American Wedding* and *American Reunion*, for instance, *American Retirement* might have comedic potential. And there are, of course, incredible gross-out possibilities in...*American Funeral*.

Notes

1 The National Lampoon 'Vacation' series comprises *National Lampoon's Vacation* (Ramis, 1983), *National Lampoon's European Vacation* (Heckerling, 1985) and *National Lampoon's Christmas Vacation* (Chechik, 1989).
2 Critics such as John Bynner (2005), however, observe that Arnett's claims for the universality of 'emergent adulthood' fail to recognise both significant national variations and a huge diversity in individual experience.
3 Much of the humour derives from the way comedian Burke – a squat, middle-aged woman – plays Perry, an achingly gauche teenage boy.
4 This difference may partially account for the failure of a US version of *The Inbetweeners* TV series. Sitcoms premised on class tensions have seldom fared well in the US and, after debuting on MTV in 2012, the American incarnation of *The Inbetweeners* was soon scrapped.
5 There are three Harold & Kumar releases – *Harold & Kumar Go to White Castle* (Leiner, 2004), *Harold & Kumar Escape from Guantanamo Bay* (Hurwitz and Scholssberg, 2008) and *A Very Harold & Kumar 3D Christmas* (Hurwitz and Schlossberg, 2011). They were all written by Jon Hurwitz and Hayden Schlossberg, who would go on to write and direct American Pie's fourth theatrical release, *American Reunion*.
6 As many critics noted, the plot echoed that for 2007's *Superbad*.

Bibliography

'A New $10-Billion Power: The US Teenage Consumer'. (1959) *Life*, 31 August, pp. 78–85.

Abrams, N. (2012) *The New Jew: Exploring Jewishness and Judaism in Contemporary Cinema*, London: I.B. Tauris.

Altman, R. (1999) *Film/Genre*, London: British Film Institute.

Arkoff, S. (1997) *Flying through Hollywood by the Seat of My Pants*, Secaucus, NJ: Carol Publishing.

Arnett, J. (2004) *Emerging Adulthood: The Winding Road from the Late Teens through the Twenties*, Oxford: Oxford University Press.

Austin, B. (1985) 'The Development and Decline of the Drive-In Movie Theater', in Austin, B. (ed.) *Current Research in Film: Audiences, Economics and Law Vol. 1*, Norwood, NJ: Ablex, pp. 59–92.

Bakhtin, M. (1984) *Rabelais and His World*, Bloomington: Indiana University Press (H. Iswolsky, translated).

Balchack, B. (2006) '*American Pie Band Camp* Marches to the #1 DVD Slot', *MovieWeb*, online, 6 January, https://movieweb.com/american-pie-band-camp-marches-to-the-1-dvd-slot/ (accessed 13 June 2019).

Barton, E. (2011) 'Stifler from *American Pie* Was Inspired By Fort Lauderdale Man Now Charged in Fishtails Murder', *Broadward Palm Beach New Times*, online, 22 April, www.browardpalmbeach.com/music/stifler-from-american-pie-was-inspired-by-fort-lauderdale-man-now-charged-in-fishtales-murder-6429045 (accessed 5 May 2019).

Bender, A. (2012) 'Top 10 Funniest Movies Ever (As Measured in Laughs Per Minute)', *Forbes*, online, 21 September, www.forbes.com/sites/andrewbender/2012/09/21/top-10-funniest-movies-ever-as-measured-in-laughs-per-minute/#7cff6973c40e (accessed 6 April 2019).

Bernstein, J. (1997) *Pretty in Pink: The Golden Age of Teenage Movies*, New York: St Martin's Griffin.

Best, A. (2000) *Prom Night: Youth, Schools, and Popular Culture*, London: Routledge.

Bourdieu, P. (1984) *Distinction: A Social Critique of the Judgement of Taste*, London: Routledge (R. Nice, translated).

Butler, J. (1990) *Gender Trouble: Feminism and the Subversion of Identity*, London: Routledge.

Butler, J. (1993) *Bodies That Matter*, London: Routledge.

Bynner, J. (2005) 'Rethinking the Youth Phase of the Life-Course: The Case for Emerging Adulthood', *Journal of Youth Studies*, Vol. 8, No. 4, pp. 367–84.

Chartsurfer.de. (2019) 'Jahrescharts Deutschland', *Chartsurfer.de.*, online, www.chartsurfer.de/film/kinocharts-deutschland/charts-2000 (accessed 10 April 2019).

Chase, S. (2018) 'Another *American Pie* Film Will Happen – According to Tara Reid', *Digital Spy*, online, 3 August, www.digitalspy.com/movies/a863108/tara-reid-american-pie-five/ (accessed 10 March 2019).

Clover, C. (1992) *Men, Women, and Chainsaws: Gender in the Modern Horror Film*, Princeton, NJ: Princeton University Press.

Cohan, S. and Hark, I.R. (1993) 'Introduction', in Cohan, S. and Hark, I.R. (eds) *Screening the Male: Exploring Masculinities in Hollywood Cinema*, London: Routledge, pp. 1–8.

Collin, R. (2014) '*The Inbetweeners 2* and the Teen Sex Comedy Renaissance', *The Telegraph*, online, 10 August, www.telegraph.co.uk/culture/film/11021355/The-Inbetweeners-2-and-the-teen-sex-comedy-renaissance.html (accessed 13 February 2019).

Connell, R.W. (1995) *Masculinities*, Berkeley: University of California Press.

Coy, B. (2017) 'The Moment that Made *American Pie* a Hit', *The Chronicle*, online, 13 June, www.thechronicle.com.au/news/moment-made-american-pie-hit/3189040/ (accessed 15 March 2019).

Crook, S. (ed.) (2000) 'The 50 Greatest Comedies Ever!', *Total Film*, November, pp. 49–77.

Davis, N.Z. (1965) 'Women On Top', in Davis, N.Z. (ed.) *Society and Culture in Early Modern France: Eight Essays*, Stanford, CA: Stanford University Press, pp. 124–51.

De Vaney, A. (2002) 'Pretty in Pink? John Hughes Re-inscribes Daddy's Girl in Homes and Schools', in Pomerance, M. and Gateward, F. (eds) *Sugar, Spice and Everything Nice: Cinemas of Girlhood*, Detroit, MI: Wayne State University Press, pp. 201–16.

Denby, D. (1999) 'Film Review: *American Pie*', *The New Yorker*, 12 July.

Docker, J. (1994) *Postmodernism and Popular Culture: A Cultural History*, Cambridge: Cambridge University Press.

Doherty, T. (2002) *Teenagers and Teenpics: The Juvenilization of American Movies in the 1950s*, 2nd ed., Philadelphia, PA: Temple University Press.

Driscoll, C. (2011) *Teen Film: A Critical Introduction*, Oxford: Berg.

Eco, U. (1984) 'The Frames of Comic "Freedom"', in Sebok, T. (ed.) *Carnival!*, Berlin: Mouton, pp. 1–9.

Fenster, B. (1999) 'Film Review: *American Pie*', *Arizona Republic*, 9 July.

Fiske, J. (1989) *Understanding the Popular*, Boston, MA: Unwin Hyman.

Glynn, K. (2000) *Tabloid Culture: Trash Taste, Popular Power, and the Transformation of American Television*, Durham, NC: Duke University Press.

Going, A. (2018) '15 Secrets You Didn't Know Behind The *American Pie Franchise*', *Screen Rant*, online, 17 February, https://screenrant.com/american-pie-movies-hidden-behind-secrets-trivia/ (accessed 23 February 2019).

Grainge, P. (2000) 'Nostalgia and Style in Retro America: Moods, Modes and Media Recycling', *Journal of American and Comparative Culture*, Vol. 23, No. 1, pp. 27–35.

Grant, B. K. (2007) *Film Genre: From Iconography to Ideology*, New York: Wallflower Press.

Greven, D. (2002) 'Dude, Where's My Gender?: Contemporary Teen Comedies and New Forms of American Masculinity', *Cineaste*, Vol. 27, No. 3, pp. 14–21.

Guerrasio, Jason. (2019) 'How *Booksmart* Went from a 2009 Script Collecting Dust to This Year's Must-See Movie of the Summer', *Business Insider*, online, 25 May, www.businessinsider.com/booksmart-from-hyped-2009-script-to-a-2019-hit-movie-2019-5?r=US&IR=T (accessed 28 May 2019).

Hendra, T. (1987) *Going Too Far: The Rise and Demise of Sick, Gross, Black, Sophomoric, Weirdo, Pinko, Anarchist, Underground, Anti-Establishment Humor*, New York: Doubleday.

Hentges, S. (2006) *Pictures of Girlhood: Modern Female Adolescence on Film*, Jefferson, NC: McFarland.

Holden, S. (1999) 'Film Review: The Road to Manhood, Paved in Raunchy Jokes and Pie', *New York Times*, 9 July.

Horten, R. (1999) 'Film Review: *American Pie*', *Film.com*, online, 6 August; cited on *Metacritic*, online, www.metacritic.com/movie/american-pie/critic-reviews (accessed 15 February 2019).

Hutcheon, L. (1989) *The Politics of Postmodernism*, London: Routledge.

Jameson, F. (1985) 'Postmodernism and Consumer Society', in Foster, H. (ed.) *The Anti-Aesthetic: Essays on Post-Modern Culture*, Seattle: Bay Press: 111–25.

Jameson, F. (1991) *Postmodernism, or the Cultural Logic of Late Capitalism*, Durham, NC: Duke University Press.

Jeffords, S. (1989) *The Remasculinization of America: Gender and the Vietnam War*, Bloomington: Indiana University Press.

Kaveney, R. (2006) *Teen Dreams: Reading Teen Film and Television from Heathers to Veronica Mars*, London: I.B. Tauris.

Kearney, M.C. (2002) 'Girlfriends and Girl Power: Female Adolescence in Contemporary U.S. Cinema', in Gatewood, F. and Pomerance, M. (eds) *Sugar, Spice, and Everything Nice: Cinemas of Girlhood*, Detroit: Wayne State University Press, pp. 125–44.

Kendall, L. (1999) 'Nerd Nation: Images of Nerds in US Popular Culture', *International Journal of Cultural Studies*, Vol. 2, No. 2, pp. 260–83.

Kidd, K. (2004) 'He's Gotta Have It: Teen Film as Sex Education', in Nelson, C. and Martin, M. (eds), *Sexual Pedagogies: Sex Education in Britain, Australia and America*, Basingstoke: Palgrave, pp. 95–112.

King, G. (2002) *Film Comedy*, London: Wallflower Press.

Klein, A. (2011) *American Film Cycles: Reframing Genres, Screening Social Problems, and Defining Subcultures*, Austin: University of Texas Press.

Leigh, D. (1999) 'Film Review: The Pie Who Loved Me', *The Guardian*, on-line, 1 October, www.theguardian.com/film/1999/oct/01/2 (accessed 5 February 2019).

Macdonald, D. (1958) 'A Caste, a Culture, a Market', *New Yorker*, 22 November, pp. 57–94.

Maher, K. (n.d.) 'Film Review: *American Pie*', *BFI: Film Forever*, online, http:// old.bfi.org.uk/sightandsound/review/209 (accessed 20 February 2019).

Mathijs, E. and Sexton, J. (2011) *Cult Cinema: An Introduction*, Oxford: Wiley-Blackwell.

Medhurst, A. (1986) 'Music Hall and British Cinema', in Barr, C. (ed.) *All Our Yesterdays: 90 Years of British Cinema*, London: BFI, pp. 168–88.

Merck, M. (2007) '*American Pie* 1999', in Merck, M. (ed.) *America First: Naming the Nation in US Film*, New York: Routledge, pp. 259–76.

Modell, J. (1989) *Into One's Own: From Youth to Adulthood in the United States 1920–1975*, Berkeley: University of California Press.

Moyer, J. (2015) 'Gloomy Don McLean Reveals Meaning of "American Pie" – and Sells Lyrics for $1.2 Million', *The Washington Post*, online 8 April, www.washingtonpost.com/news/morning-mix/wp/2015/04/08/gloomy-don-mclean-reveals-meaning-of-american-pie-and-sells-lyrics-for-1-2-million/?noredirect=on&utm_term=.1f756e538431 (accessed 15 May 2019).

Mulvey, L. (1975) 'Visual Pleasure and Narrative Cinema', *Screen*, Vol. 16, No. 3, Autumn, pp. 6–18.

Myers, S. (2014) 'Script to Screen: *American Pie*', *Go Into the History*, online, 27 August, https://gointothestory.blcklst.com/script-to-screen-american-pie-20c97cf1fba4 (accessed 13 February 2019).

Nashway, C. (1999) 'Pie in Your Face: It's Hot Time, Summer in the Cinema', *Entertainment Weekly*, 16 July, p. 26.

Neale, S. (2000) *Genre and Hollywood*, London: Routledge.

Nowell, R. (2011) *Blood Money: A History of the First Teen Slasher Film Cycle*, London: Continuum.

Noxon, C. (2006) *Rejuvenile: Kickball, Cartoons, Cupcakes, and the Reinvention of the American Grown-Up*, New York: Crown.

Otto, J. (2003) 'A Conversation with Adam Herz', *IGN*, online, 31 July, https:// uk.ign.com/articles/2003/07/31/a-conversation-with-adam-herz (accessed 20 March 2019).

Paul, W. (1994) *Laughing Screaming: Modern Hollywood Horror and Comedy*, New York: Columbia University Press.

Parish, J. (2000) *Jason Biggs: Hollywood's Newest Cutie-Pie!*, New York: St. Marten's Press.

Pearce S. (2003) '"As Wholesome As...": *American Pie* as a New Millennium Sex Manual', in Mallan, K. and Pearce, S. (eds) *Youth Cultures: Texts, Images, and Identities*, London: Praeger, pp. 69–80.

Pfefferman, N. (2001) 'A Jewish Slice of *American Pie*', *Jewish Journal*, online, 9 August, https://jewishjournal.com/culture/arts/4673/ (accessed 17 February 2019).

Pokorny, M., Miskell, P. and Sedgwick, J. (2019) 'Managing Uncertainty in Creative Industries: Film Sequels and Hollywood's Profitability, 1988–2015', *Competition & Change*, Vol. 23, No. 1, pp. 23–46.

'Porky's' (2019) *The Numbers*, online, www.the numbers.com/movie/Porkys#tab=summary (accessed 5 March 2019).

Quail, C. (2011) 'Nerds, Geeks, and the Hip/Square Dialectic in Contemporary Television', *Television and New Media*, Vol. 12, No. 5, pp. 460–82.

Radish, C. (2012) 'Writer/Directors Jon Hurwitz and Hayden Schlossberg Talk *American Reunion*', *Collider*, online 26 March, http://collider.com/american-reunion-jon-hurwitz-hayden-schlossberg-interview/ (accessed 15 February 2019).

Roth, P. (1969) *Portnoy's Complaint*, New York: Random House.

Rowe, K. (1995) *The Unruly Woman: Gender and the Genres of Laughter*, Austin: University of Texas Press.

Saxton, M. (1992/1974) 'Philip Roth Talks about His Own Work', in Searles, G. (ed.) *Conversations with Philip Roth*, Jackson: University Press of Mississippi, pp. 77–80.

'Saying Bye-Bye to a Big Slice of *American Pie*'. (2000) *Los Angeles Times,* 22 February.

Schaefer, E. (1999) *'Bold! Daring! Shocking! True!': A History of Exploitation Films, 1919–1959*, Durham, NC: Duke University Press.

Segrave, K. (2006) *Drive-In Theaters: A History from Their Inception in 1933*, 2nd ed., Jefferson, NC: McFarland & Co.

Shary, T. (1996) 'The Only Place to Go Is Inside: Confusions about Sexuality and Class in *Clueless* and *Kids*', in Pomerance, M. and Sakeris, J. (eds) *Pictures of a Generation on Hold*, Toronto: Ryerson Polytechnic University, pp. 157–66.

Shary, T. (2005) *Teen Movies: American Youth on Screen*, London: Wallflower Press.

Shary, T. (2007) 'Introduction: Youth Culture Shock', in Shary, T. and Seibel, A. (eds), *Youth Culture in Global Cinema*, Austin: University of Texas Press, pp. 1–6.

Shary, T. (2014) *Generation Multiplex: The Image of Youth in American Cinema Since 1980*, 2nd ed., Austin: University of Texas Press.

Siegel, R. (2012) 'The Story Behind *American Pie*', *Blu-Ray.Com*, online, 16 March, www.blu-ray.com/news/?id=8343 (accessed 16 February 2019).

Simpson, M. (1994) *Male Impersonators: Men Performing Masculinity*, London: Cassell.

Smith, F. (2017) *Rethinking the Hollywood Teen Movie*, Edinburgh: Edinburgh University Press.

Speed, L. (2010) 'Loose Cannons: White Masculinity and the Vulgar Teen Comedy Film', *Journal of Popular Culture*, Vol. 43, No. 4, pp. 820–41.

Speed, L. (2018) *Clueless: American Youth in the 1990s*, London: Routledge.

Stam, R. (1992) *Subversive Pleasures: Bakhtin, Cultural Criticism, and Film*, Baltimore, MD: Johns Hopkins University Press.

Steinberg, S. and Kincheloe, J. (1998) 'Privileged and Getting Away With It: The Cultural Studies of White, Middle-Class Youth', *Studies in the Literary Imagination*, Vol. 31, No. 1, pp. 103–26.

Storey, J. (2001) 'The Sixties in the Nineties: Pastiche or Hyperconsciousness?', in Osgerby, B. and Gough-Yates, A. (eds) *Action TV: Tough Guys, Smooth Operators and Foxy Chicks*, London: Routledge, pp. 236–50.

Taylor, J. (2018) 'People Re-watching *American Pie* Are Getting Seriously Offended', *VT*, online, 27 February, http://vt.co/entertainment/film-tv/people-re-watching-american-pie-getting-seriously-offended?utm_source=vt&utm_medium=junglecreations&utm_campaign=post (accessed 5 May 2019).

'The Colossal Drive-In' (1957) *Newsweek*, 22 July, pp. 50 and 85.

'*The Kentucky Fried Movie*' (2019) *The Numbers,* online, www.the-numbers.com/movie/Kentucky-Fried-Movie-The#tab=summary (accessed 5 March 2019).

Thiessen, R. (1998) 'Deconstructing Masculinity in *Porky's*', *Post Script*, Vol. 18, No. 2, Winter/Spring, pp. 64–74.

Travers, P. (1999) 'Film Review: *American Pie*', *Rolling Stone*, 8 July.

Thompson, D. (2017) *Hit Makers: How Things Become Popular*, London: Allen Lane.

TRU (2002) 'Teens Spent $172 Billion in 2001', Teen Research Unlimited, Press Release, 25 January.

Tzioumakis, Y. (2006) *American Independent Cinema: An Introduction*, Edinburgh: Edinburgh University Press.

'Universal May Have Egg on Face after Selling Foreign Rights to *Pie*' (1999), *Los Angeles Times*, 8 June.

U.S. Bureau of Census (2001) *Census 2000*, Washington, DC: US Department of Commerce, Economics and Statistics Administration.

Viacom Brand Solutions International (2008) *The Golden Age of Youth*, New York: Viacom Brand Solutions International.

Waterman, D. (2005) *Hollywood's Road to Riches*, Cambridge, MA: Harvard University Press.

Watson, P. (1997) 'There's No Accounting for Taste: Exploitation Cinema and the Limits of Film Theory', in Cartmell, D., Hunter, I.Q., Kay, H. and Wheleyan, I. (eds) *Trash Aesthetics: Popular Culture and Its Audience*, London: Pluto Press, pp. 66–87.

Williams, A. (2002) 'Introduction', in Williams, A. (ed.) *Film and Nationalism*, London: Rutgers University Press, pp. 1–24.

Wood, R. (2003) 'Teens, Parties, and Rollercoasters: A Genre of the 1990s', in Wood, R. (ed.) *Hollywood from Vietnam to Reagan… and Beyond*, New York: Columbia University Press, pp. 309–32.

Wyatt, J. (1994) *High Concept: Movies and Marketing in Hollywood*, Austin: University of Texas Press.

Index

Note: *Italic* page numbers refer to figures and page numbers followed by "n" denote endnotes.